"There is a place at Roads End called the Big Six. Whenever I run my dogs I go there and think about choices I have made in my life. As the sound of the dogs barking echoes through the trees, I rest my mind and listen to the sounds of nature and imagine what it must have been like when my grandfather hunted these same woods before me. As the warmth of the sun hits my face and the dogs go silent, I hear my family and friends calling me to make another drive with the dogs."

— Jimbo Carter

ROADS END

ROADS END

G.W. Reynolds III

Rutledge Books, Inc.  Danbury, CT

This is a work of fiction. While, as in all fiction, the literary perceptions and insights are based on experience, all names, characters, places and incidents are either products of the author's imagination or are used fictitiously. No reference to any real person is intended or should be inferred.

Cover artwork and illustrations by Barbara Holmes

Copyright © 2001 by G.W. Reynolds III

ALL RIGHTS RESERVED

Rutledge Books, Inc.
107 Mill Plain Road, Danbury, CT 06811
1-800-278-8533
www.rutledgebooks.com

Manufactured in the United States of America

Cataloging in Publication Data
Reynolds, G.W., III.

   Roads End

   ISBN: 1-58244-191-X

   1. Fiction.

Library of Congress Control Number: 2001093827

Thanks to Dr. Bill Wood for his inspiration and the other Roads End members for allowing us to use the hunting camp as the setting and background for this fictitious novel and illustrations.

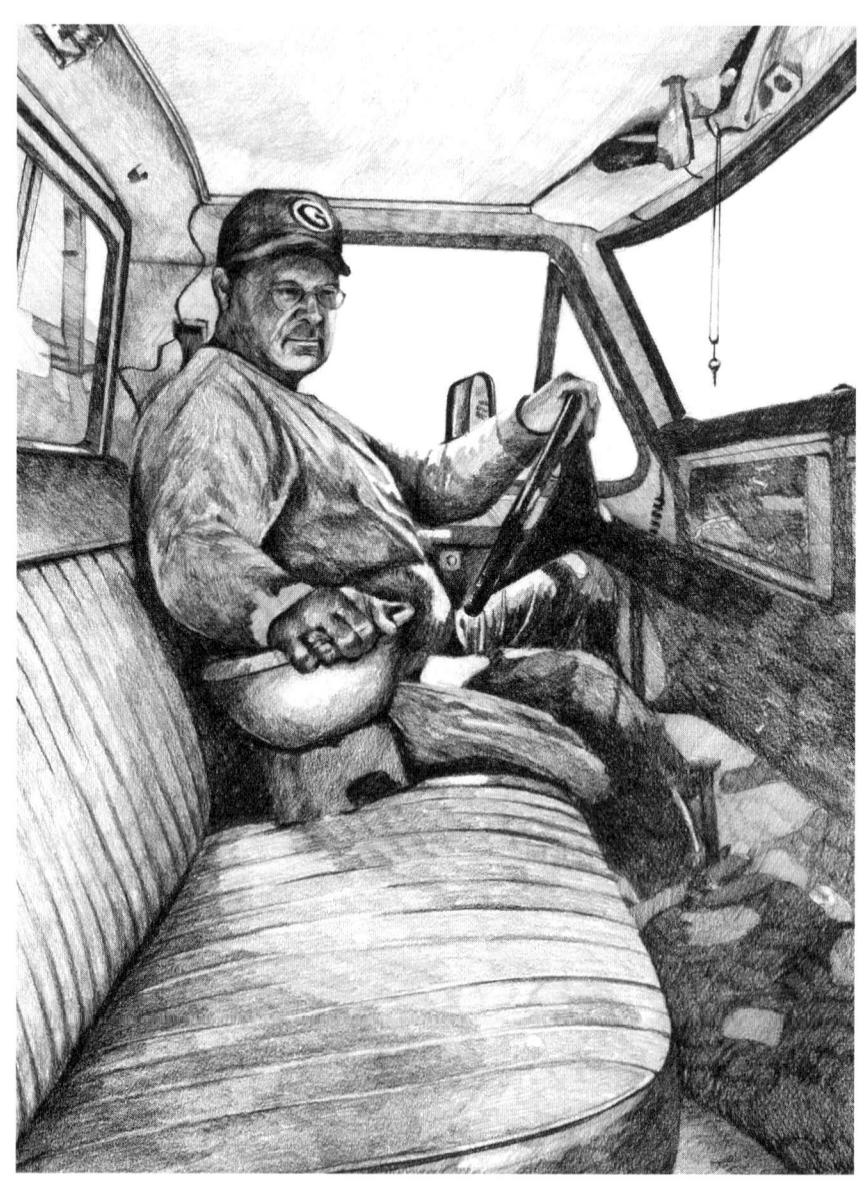

Leon Barrett

Leon Barrett had to use what driving skills he had to keep his truck from sliding off the rocks of the old railroad track hunting road. He was glad he wasn't fighting the wet clay on No-Go Road, but the small slippery rocks were giving him enough of a challenge. It was hard enough to control any vehicle on the small rocks at a slow speed, but an attempt to drive the seven miles at forty miles an hour was just ridiculous. He was also hampered by the fact he kept taking his eyes off the road to talk to the large Tupperware bowl on the front seat next to him.

"How the hell did I end up with you in my truck?" He looked away from the bowl and continued his struggle with the rocky road and a shaking steering wheel. One mistake and he would be in one of the water filled ditches on either side of the old tram road. Leon's biceps and forearms were flexed as he tried to keep the wheel straight on the steering column. He tried not to look at the plastic bowl next to him, but he couldn't help it.

"You know Jim, they're gonna be real mad if I don't get you there on time. And you know I didn't want to be your babysitter." Leon looked out the front window and kept talking.

"Hell, I don't even like you as much as the rest of 'em do. This is crazy." Leon kept his left hand on the steering wheel and put his other hand on top of the container.

"I ought'a throw your ass right out that damn window. But somebody would probably shoot me durin' the night if I don't bring ya in." The small rocks bounced off the bottom of the truck as Leon kept moving forward. He licked his dry lips and had more to say to the bowl.

"I was the butt of more of your stupid jokes than anybody else out there. I didn't think any of 'em were funny. I was an easy mark 'cause I've always been too trustin' of folks. You sure broke me of that flaw. You must'a seen me comin' right away. I was an easy fish for a fooler like you." Leon fought the road for a second and then kept talking.

"Wait a minute now, I do have to give you credit for teachin' all those kids to drive. That old truck of yours did teach a lot of boys to drive. You could see how exciting it was for them to be sittin' up in that front seat behind the wheel of your ol' stick shift. Why'd ya do that, Jim; take up all that time with all them little snot noses? You were a strange one, I'll say that about ya." Leon shook his head and gripped the steering wheel even harder as the truck began to slide off the road. Leon realized he couldn't hold the truck on the road as it slid sideways and the back wheels left the rock filled road.

"Hold on, Jim, we're goin' in the drink." Leon braced himself with his left arm and reached for the Tupperware bowl. It was gone from its' resting spot on the seat. The front wheels left the road and splashed into the water-filled ditch on the passenger side of the truck. Leon's size and strength kept him from flying through the front windshield. The quick stop jarred his body, but he was not injured. His arms would be sore later, but he wouldn't mention his discomfort to anyone.

Leon looked out the front window and focused his eyes on the water that covered the hood of the truck. Then he thought out loud to himself, "Jim"! He looked on the seat and Jim was gone. Leon slid his body over toward the passenger door and stuck his head down to the floorboard. His eyes opened wide when he saw that the Tupperware bowl had fallen to the floor and the top had popped off. The cremated remains of Jim Mott lay on the floor of Leon Barrett's truck.

"Holy shit, Jim, I thought them bowls was spill proof. I burped it and everything to seal it air tight. I guess they don't mean they stay sealed in a truck wreck. Damn, they're really gonna be mad 'bout this. How in the hell did I get here with you?"

Leon reached for the bowl on the floor and scooped up as much of the ashes as he could as he picked the bowl up. About half of Jim Mott was in the bowl with the rest of him still on the floor. Leon took the lid and scooped up as much of the other half as he could. He shook his head as he put the bowl up on the dashboard. "I could use that dust buster the boys gave Margaret for Christmas right now and I'd suck your ass right off that floor. I knew you was gonna find a way to cause me grief, dead or alive." Leon put the top back on the bowl and held it up. "Hell, they ain't gonna know some of ya's missin'." Leon opened the door on the driver's side of the truck and crawled out holding the remains of Jim Mott under his big arm. His boots sunk into the soft, wet bank of the ditch, but he kept his feet as he climbed to the rock covered train road. Leon looked down at the road ahead of him and Jim.

"Well, I figure we got about a three mile walk before the gate. We're already late. If they don't like it, they can all kiss my ass." Leon looked down at the Tupperware bowl he was holding. "And you can kiss it, too."

Bill Wood opened the screen door and stepped outside onto a concrete slab. His soon to be thirteen year old son, John, followed his father out into the front yard. A group of dogs began to bark from their pen when they saw their two masters. Bill put his big hand on John's head. "They'll all be coming in soon, son. It feels good to be the first ones here, doesn't it? I like being the official welcoming committee. It's a true honor for us both, always remember that." John wasn't paying much attention to his father's words of wisdom, but he did look up and smile as he kicked a big bull frog off the concrete slab and into the yard. Bill watched the frog bounce a few times in the dirt and then disappear under his 1963 Volkswagen bug. Bill turned to John.

"Don't let Coach Barrett see you kick that good, he'll try to have you kicking field goals for those Georgia Bulldogs." John smiled again and ran toward the dog pen where the dogs were still causing a commotion.

"Let 'em be, son. They're just as excited as we are. They can sense it, too. It's like Christmas Eve, none of us will sleep tonight." John knelt down at the dog pen as the five dogs stuck their black noses through the squares of the fence. John touched all five noses, as the dogs barked, wagged their tails and fought to gain the advantaged position for John's attention. "You fella's can't bark all night. You gotta be quiet later, so get it all out of your system before it gets dark." When Bill Wood was not hunting he was a family man and optometrist in Jacksonville, Florida. Most folks called him Doc Wood.

A loud and strange blast from a horn blew in the distance. Bill and John both looked in the direction of the strange noise and saw an old green open-sided Jeep coming into view as it passed through the main gate. The old Jeep was equipped with a compressor to blow a huge diesel truck horn just like the eighteen wheelers had. Bill knew it was his friend, Luther Reynolds. Bill also knew it would take Luther a while to drive from the main gate. As a lawman, he would never break the speed limit unless he was in a high speed pursuit and he hadn't been in one of those for years. As chief of police in Duval County, Florida, he wasn't involved in many high speed chases. Luther was one of the most senior and respected members. The slow moving Jeep pulled up to the front door and Luther, wearing his camouflaged hat, stuck his head and cigar out of the driver's side of the Jeep.

"You seen any pissbirds around here?" Bill grinned at his old friend.

"No sir, not yet, but I'd bet money there will be a flock of 'em before nightfall." Luther smiled and took the big cigar out of his mouth, blowing a mass of smoke into the air. "Ain't it funny how those damn pissbirds seem to come around these parts this time each year. How the hell are ya, Bill?"

"I'm good, sir. I'm always good when I'm here. You look ready, sir."

"Damn straight, I'm ready. I missed you boys." Luther got out of the Jeep as Bill stepped up to greet him with a firm, manly handshake and a respectful hug. Real men don't mind a hug of respect. Luther stepped back and took a deep breath.

"I've always liked the smell of sulfur water. We had sulfur water at home when I was a boy. Folks say it stinks. I think it smells like lilac water. A woman gets out of a sulfur water bath with me near by, I'll tear her towel off with my teeth, that is, what's left of 'em." Bill smiled at Luther's walk down memory lane or perhaps fantasy lane. His old friend always seemed to have interesting thoughts in his seventy-five year old head. Luther looked over Bill's shoulder and spotted John looking at him from the dog pen.

"Don't tell me that's John?" Bill smiled that big proud smile of his, the same one he always smiled when John was the subject.

"Yes sir, that's him." Luther shook his head.

"They grow way to fast, don't they? I'm gettin' older every day. I feel it and I hate it."

Bill wasn't sure how to respond to Luther's comment, but Luther didn't seem to want a response. He had a serious question.

"Mott here yet?" Bill shook his head.

"Not yet, sir. Leon's bringing him in." Luther's eyes opened as wide as they could.

"Leon! What the hell is he doin' with Jim?"

"I'm not quite sure how he got the responsibility, but he did. I'm sure he'll be here."

Leon Barrett sat down on a tree stump and put the Tupperware bowl on the ground next to him. He took one of his boots off. "My damn socks are wet and rolled down to my toes." Leon pulled his sock up and put his boot back on. He did the same with the other boot and sock and kept talking to the bowl. "I really thought we'd be there before dark, but now I ain't so sure. That sun's droppin' awful fast. We should'a took the other way in. I can't think clear with you sittin' next to me, like you ain't dead. You always get me flustered. If we was on the other road somebody would'a come by and picked us up by now. I just know you've got a hand in all this, somehow." Leon stood up, picked up the bowl and walked back to the road.

Four more trucks were parked near the front concrete slab and two trucks were parked near the dog pens. The two trucks near the pens had more barking dogs in cages lashed to the back flat beds. James Reynolds, Dallas Thomas, Leonard Hooks, and Big John Blanyer all stood on the concrete slab with Bill Wood and Luther Reynolds. Malcolm Johnson, Lonnie Sikes and Jimmy Carter were at the dog pens taking dogs out of their trucks and putting them into different pens. Jimmy Carter had one whole pen full of his usual thirty dogs. James Reynolds stood in front of Bill Wood and had the same question on his mind.

"Jim Mott here?" Bill shook his head again.

"Not yet, but he's on the way." Luther couldn't resist.

The Camp

"Leon's bringin' him in." All eyes turned to Bill. James Reynolds still had the floor.

"Do you think that was such a good idea, Bill?" Bill felt all ten eyeballs glaring at him.

"I don't know how Leon got picked for the job. I didn't pick him. Hell, the funeral was three weeks ago." James' eyes lit up again.

"You mean to say, he's been with Butch for three weeks?"

"I don't know when Leon picked him up, or even why. Maybe, in all our sadness, we left and nobody thought about what we had to do. Leon must have been the last one there or came by later and then somebody in the family remembered about us. That's all I can figure. Let's give Leon the chance to come through."

James Reynolds loved Leon Barrett like he was his own son. It was a fact that James was more a father to Leon than his real father. The man that Leon had become was because of James Reynolds' efforts and his philosophy of life, which he shared openly with the man he almost always called Butch. James knew Leon was a strange pick to be hauling the remains of Jim Mott all over the county, because he also knew Jim Mott and Leon didn't see eye-to-eye on many occasions. This made Leon an unusual pick to bring Jim in that night.

Leon Barrett leaned against a fence post with no fence hooked to it. He put the Tupperware bowl down on the ground next to the post. "Now, this whole thing is really startin' to make me mad. I know we're goin' in the right direction. I should'a stayed on the road, but I just knew it was through these woods." Leon looked down at the bowl. "You should'a said somethin'. Any other time, you'd be given me orders and directions and tellin' everybody what to do." The sun was gone from the sky.

There was a small army of men in the front yard. Trucks were parked everywhere. There was enough visible fire power in that front yard to invade Brunswick, if need be. They looked like they were getting ready to go to war. With the horns blowing, dogs barking and men laughing, the noise level was deafening. Bill Wood looked out into the yard and smiled his biggest smile of all. He spotted his son, John, helping the other men unload their equipment from the trucks. Bill Wood loved the sights, sounds and smells on the eve of the official hunting season.

Leon Barrett could hear the noises through the woods ahead of him. He knew he would soon deliver the package that had fallen into his care. He held up the Tupperware bowl close to his face. "I'll be glad to hand your ass over to the others. This ain't been my idea of the way I wanted to begin this huntin' season. This is a bad omen and I probably should drop you off and get the hell out of here." Even though Leon had said that out loud, he knew he wouldn't tell anyone he had his doubts about what was to come.

The building was full of men dressed in their hunting attire. They carried their blankets, pillows, boxes, suitcases and duffle bags into the barrack type bedrooms. Each room had two sets of bunk beds. Every old man and every young man was doing his part to unload the trucks, put away the supplies and prepare the rooms. Bill Wood was making sure each new arrival was greeted properly and welcomed with a firm handshake and a smile. He would find his son, John, to keep an eye on him and be sure he was doing his part, but mainly to be sure John was O.K. Bill felt immense pride each time he would see John helping the older hunters with their equipment and supplies. John would be thirteen the next morning and being with his father, for the first day of hunting season, was to honor his birthday.

Leon Barrett could see the truck lights through the woods. He still held the bowl containing the remains of Jim Mott under his big arm. His journey would soon end and the responsibility that had been bestowed upon him would be lifted. He stepped up his pace as he walked toward the lights.

John Wood stood near the dog pens with his hands over both ears. He had counted seventy-three dogs and they had all been barking from the moment they were put into the pens. John's head was on a swivel and his, soon to be thirteen year old eyes, were absorbing every movement in the yard around him. At that moment there was no more exciting place on earth. It was like a wild dream in full Technicolor and the action was centered around him. The young man had no idea his father was watching him again from the front door of the building. Big John Blanyer stepped up behind Bill Wood at the door.

"Don't worry 'bout that boy of your's. He'll be fine." Bill smiled and turned to his friend.

"I know. I just like looking at him." Big John patted Bill on the back as they both walked back into the building. Big John had the same question that was on everybody's mind.

"When's Leon comin' with Mott?"

The room went silent and all eyes were on Bill. It was as if they had all asked the same question at the same time. Bill looked around the room, focusing in on a few of the individual faces he had known for years. Bill shook his head and gave a half smile. "Damn, fellas, there are some ugly men in this room." About half the men laughed at Bill's humor, but the ugly men didn't. Ugly folks usually know who they are. They don't act like they know, but they know. James Reynolds wouldn't let Bill change the subject. "Let's get back to the question about Leon and Mott."

Leon Barrett stood at the front gate. He could see the trucks, the few men still standing around, those working outside, and he could hear the dogs. Even though he would never say it to anyone, he was relieved to be standing there and he would complete his mission in a matter of minutes. To his left he could see pieces of the burned and charred wood from the original camp that mysteriously burned a few years before. The original building was a patchwork of wood siding, tin roof, broken window panes and torn window screens. The windows had been broken because one of Bill Wood's more interesting guests threw an eight inch missile, actually a land mine simulator, on the ground outside next to the building as a funny way to wake everyone up. The concussion of the explosion did the damage to the windows and the noise was heard for miles around.

Most of the sleeping members ran outside thinking it was a serious train wreck. Senses of humors do differ. It would sleep only ten men and had no shower or hot water. Bathing was done with a garden hose near the outside well. There was one toilet and one sink. The old camp had hundreds of holes in the wooden floor because the Carter brothers, Donny and Jimmy, used to shoot holes in the floor after they had hosed down the floors and walls with soap and water. The more holes, the faster the soapy water drained off, under the building.

The new lodge could sleep forty-two men, had double toilets, urinals, sinks and showers and was four times bigger than the original building. It was truly a worthwhile fire. There was only one strange, thoughtless construction design and that was the installation of a large steel drain cover on the concrete floor of the main hallway entrance.

Jim Mott enjoyed scaring everybody by spinning the steel cover, making an awful noise much worse than the noise of the train going by. Tom Cravey was the member who had the good sense to bolt that noisy drain cover to the floor. Leon Barrett pushed the unlocked gate open and along with Jim Mott, stepped into the world of the Roads End hunting camp.

Once again the room was silent. Bill Wood knew they were worried about Leon and Jim Mott, not necessarily in that order. Luther Reynolds had his own question.

"Did anybody call to see if he even has Mott with him?" Bill Wood was glad somebody asked a question he could answer. "Leon's had Mott in his truck for three weeks. He got him the night of the funeral." Every eye in the room was wide open and there were mumbled words coming from each mouth, but it only sounded like a lot of noise. James Reynolds' voice cut through the noise, loud and clear. "Does Leon even know about Mott's wishes and are we sure he's gonna be here to hunt in the first place?"

"Somebody mention my name?" All eyes in the room turned to the voice they all recognized. Leon Barrett and Jim Mott stood as one in the doorway of Roads End.

The room exploded into cheers and laughter as the men moved and gathered around the now late and thought to be lost fellow soldier. Bill smiled with relief and the crowd opened a path as Leon strode through the men and made his way to the huge round wooden table in the middle of the room. He took the Tupperware bowl from under his arm and put it in the middle of the table. Once again, every eye was wide open as they stared at the item Leon had set before them. And once again the room was silent for a few seconds. Leon broke the silence.

"Well, there's Mott, safe and sound. We'd a been here earlier, but we had a little accident and my truck's in the ditch off the ol' rock road. We did the last three or four miles on foot, or I did it on foot. Jim didn't help much." Leon looked at the expression on all the faces around him and down at the Tupperware bowl on the table. No one had any words for another few seconds. James Reynolds couldn't contain himself. He looked directly at the large bowl.

"What the hell is that?" Leon looked at the bowl and then he looked at James.

"It's a Tupperware bowl, what the hell's it look like?" James kept his eyes on the bowl.

"I know it's a bowl, but why are Jim's ashes in a damn

Tupperware bowl? I thought when folks got cremated they put 'em in a vase or somethin'." A voice came from the crowd.

"They usually put 'em in an urn." James nodded his head. "Yeah, that's it, an urn. Why is he in this bowl?" Leon was ready to answer any questions they might have.

"He was in a jar-like thing when I first got him." The same voice came from the crowd. "That was the urn." Leon went on. " I hated leavin' him in the truck all that time. Hell y'all, I had to wait three weeks for tonight to get here." Leon looked around the room. "Anyway, to make a long story short, I broke the lid on the jar." The voice came from the crowd. "It's an urn." Leon's face went red and he pressed his lips together. "O.K. dammit, I broke the top of the urn. I went ahead and put him in one of them plastic freezer bags, but it was too creepy 'cause he looked like he belonged with the flour, or sugar. The bag was too creepy for me. Then I found the bowl. I knew it would be air tight if I burped it and I wouldn't have to worry about the top comin' off. The color of the bowl keeps it from lookin' creepy." The room now had more than a "creepy" silence to it. They were all lost for words. Leon's calm manner concerning the remains of Jim Mott had stunned them all for a moment. They were too amazed and shocked to be angry. Bill Wood knew it was time to move on.

"Leon, we thank you for taking care of Jim and getting him here to be with us and to give us the opportunity to honor his dying request. I'm sure Jim thanks you too." The sight of the bowl flying off the front seat of the truck flashed in Leon's head when he heard Bill's words. The other men mumbled as Bill stepped to the table and picked up the bowl. He held it up to the light. "Gentlemen, please welcome our good friend and fellow hunter, Jim Mott." The room exploded into cheers and talk. Leon moved away from the table as the others closed the circle around Bill and the Tupperware bowl.

The same voice came from the crowd and began a chant of respect. "Mott! Mott! Mott! Mott!" Leon stepped outside into the night as the entire room followed the chanter's lead and the night of tribute for Jim Mott had begun.

Leon Barrett stepped out of the building and stood on the concrete slab at the front door. He took a deep breath of the cool Georgia night air and felt relieved to have completed his unwanted mission. He looked down and John Wood stood in front of him. Leon smiled.

"That you, John?" John smiled too.

"Yes sir, Coach Barrett, it's me." Leon put his big hand on John's head.

"You get bigger every time I see you. When's that daddy of yours gonna let you come play ball for me and the Lee Generals?" John had a huge smile now.

"Daddy's scared you might make me a Georgia Bulldog." Leon couldn't help but laugh at the boy's honesty.

"He's sure right 'bout that. Boy, wouldn't that be somethin'. Bill Wood's boy, a black and red, hairy dawg. Yes sir, now I'd like to see that." Leon looked out at the dog pens. "Come on, John, show me your dogs."

Leon Barrett was a high school teacher and coach at Lee High School in Jacksonville, Florida. He had been hunting at Roads End with his uncle, James Reynolds, since he was nine years old. He liked working with the young men like John Wood because he knew what growing up around Roads End meant to him and he knew the other young men and boys felt the same. As a boy, Leon always liked it when the men took time to talk to him. He knew when he became a man he would take time to share moments with the future men of Roads End. Leon had brought many young men, students and athletes, from Lee High School to the doors of Roads End and he felt they were all better men because they had been there. He was also glad John Wood was there because Leon's two sons, Ed and Ramsey, would be coming to the camp. Jimmy Carter's brother, Donny, would be bringing the boys into camp from Jacksonville later that night or early in the morning. With Leon's mission to bring in Jim Mott and the ceremony to follow, he left his boys home until he could fulfill his mission.

There were ten chairs sitting around the huge round wooden table. The Tupperware bowl containing what was left of Jim Mott, still sat in the middle of the table. Bill Wood was in charge.

"Gentlemen, please take your seats and the rest of you gather 'round behind them." Nine of the men moved to sit in the chairs. Bill Wood sat down and made it an even ten seated. The standing thirty moved in and surrounded the table behind the ten chairs. Sitting at the table with Bill were: Luther Reynolds, James Reynolds, Dallas Thomas, Leonard Hooks, Big John Blanyer, T. Coy Nichols, Ned Smith, C. J. Mercer, Elbert Hysler and of course, James Henry Mott. Bill Wood knew it was only proper for the floor and the honor to go to Dallas Thomas.

The story was that the Roads End hunting camp had its beginning in 1951, when Ward Rosier threw his deed to a fifty acre tract of Glenn County, Georgia land, on a poker table to cover a final bet made by Dallas Thomas of Jacksonville, Florida. After Dallas turned over the devil red lady queen of diamonds nobody thought he had hidden, and won the pot, he promptly offered a piece of the action to each of the seven players, including Ward Rosier. Thus the Roads End hunting camp was established. The room went silent instantly when the respected, Dallas Thomas, stood up from his chair.

"Y'all know I ain't much of a talker and I'll let the others do most of it in just a minute. I just felt I should say somethin' before we honor Jim's last request." The only noise was the dogs barking outside. Actually it was rather appropriate for the occasion.

Nobody liked hearing those dogs "talking" more than Jim Mott did. Dallas continued.

"You always hear folks say things like, 'That fella walks to a different drummer', or, 'When God made him He threw away the mold', or, 'He's one of a kind'. Well, I'm here to say all those sayin's fit Jim Mott to a tee." All thirty-nine other men nodded their heads in agreement and there was mumbling in the crowd. A single voice was heard above the others. "Tell 'em 'bout Mott! Tell 'em!" The mumbling stopped and the single voice was silent. Dallas had more.

"Now, before we get to Jim's wishes, I'll ask you all to get a glass off of the counter over there." Dallas pointed toward a counter in the kitchen. "In fact, a few of y'all can pass the glasses around to everybody else." Dallas turned to the back of the room and he offered some more instructions. "Some of y'all open that box over there, take out the bottles and start pourin' that vintage Wild Turkey. It's only fittin' we taste that smooth Turkey to honor our friend and fellow Roads End hunter."

All twelve bottles of Wild Turkey were grabbed by the neck and pulled from the box. The paper seals were broken with a twist and the dark liquid began to flow into the glasses. Some let it breathe while others let it fill. Some took two fingers, some took four. Some glasses had more than others, depending on the drinker's experience, want, need or ability. Each glass had a varying amount of the hard, strong liquor. Lester Rowe was the only man holding a full bottle of Wild Turkey in his hand. But that was typical for him. Dallas waited for all the glasses to be ready. The room was silent once again and they were all standing behind the chairs. Dallas went on.

"I remember one night when we were playin' cards and Mott came in late after he had been drinkin' and dancin' at the V.F.W. The crazy bastard walked in the door, came over to the table, picked up a just opened bottle of Wild Turkey, and poured every drop into a mop bucket." A voice in the crowd said, "Sho' did." Dallas smiled. " We were all so shocked by what he did, nobody said a thing as he saluted us and went to bed. Hell, Bill was the most shaken, it was his bottle." They all laughed and there was talk for a few seconds. Bill Wood talked above the noise.

"About two weeks later, we were out on the camp road and Mott handed me a new sealed full bottle of Wild Turkey. He said he had a dream that he owed me that. We opened it and killed it right there on the spot."

Leon Barrett sat on the downed tailgate of one of the trucks parked outside. He looked toward the building and he knew the others would be deep in the world of "Mottism" for some time. John Wood had taken his father's favorite dog, Bullet, out of the pen and both boy and dog were lying on a piece of canvas in the back of Luther Reynolds' Jeep. For some strange reason the dogs had settled and only the normal deep woods sounds of the night filled the air. It was as if the dogs were also quiet in honor and respect to Jim Mott. Leon looked back at the building when he heard an explosion of laughter.

Dallas Thomas picked up his glass filled with two fingers of the liquor. He held the glass up high above his head and the other men did the same. "Gentlemen, please join me in a toast to our good friend, Jimmy Mott." Each man said, "To Jim," or "Mott,"or "Jim Mott." They all toasted him in their own way and down went the Wild Turkey. No matter what the amount in the glass, the glass would not come away from any lips until it was empty. As the nectar was gulped down, the room was filled with different animal-like noises as the different degrees of burn hit their tongues, throats and bellies. Some of the men moved away from the table to stand alone as the Turkey burn took their breath away for the moment. The more experienced and moderate drinkers kept their places at and around the table as the more daring waited for their insides to cool before they walked back to their original places. Bill Wood was in charge of the next phase of the ceremony. He blew air from his mouth as his four fingers of Turkey began to cool and he could talk again.

"Men, I'm sure Jim appreciates that fine toast. If he was here, I know he would have downed his share." A voice from the crowd said, "Sho would'a!" Bill continued.

"If y'all will now make it back to the table, please gather 'round." Bill Wood reached into his top shirt pocket and took out a shotgun shell. He stood the red shell upright on the table in front of him. The men standing around watched as the other nine men did the same and stood up a shotgun shell on the table, directly in front of each of them. Luther Reynolds was the last one to stand his shell upright. Bill continued.

"As most of you already know, Jimmy made a last request of us." A single dog howled in the front yard as if it had been cued to do so. Bill smiled, as did most of the others. "He asked that his ashes be spread to the four winds out at the Lounge."

Between deer drives, Mott would radio the other hunters and designate the crossroad where they would meet for him to assign stands and places for the dog drivers to enter the block. One such place Mott named the Lounge, because the men all seemed to lazily linger too long, talking more and hunting less while drinking beer and eating peanuts. Mott had requested that his ashes be cast to the four winds at the Lounge. Bill Wood looked at Don Crawford the camp cook and had his own request.

"Don, get the spoons." Don nodded and walked to the kitchen. Bill took his Case pocket knife out of his pants pocket and opened it, exposing the four inch blade. Each of the other nine sitting at the table took knives of various brands from their pockets too. They all began to open the end of the shotgun shell they had placed on the table in front of them. Each man was careful not to tear the fold down ends as they exposed the BBs like buckshot inside each of the red tubes. Don Crawford came back to the table carrying an opened empty can and ten table spoons. He handed the tin can to Bill Wood and placed one of the spoons on the table in front of him. Don then walked around the table placing a spoon in front of each of the others sitting at the table.

Bill Wood took his opened shotgun shell and turned it over into the tin can, dropping all the metal pellets into the can. Bill handed the can to James Reynolds and James did the same; dumping the pellets from the shell into the now filling tin can. Each man sitting at the table took his turn, doing the same with their shells, until all ten shells were emptied of pellets. Don Crawford removed the brimming can from the table.

Each of the ten men sat around the table with an empty shotgun shell casing, a table spoon and a Tupperware bowl containing Jim Mott's ashes. There was a small amount of low conversation in the room until Bill Wood stood up from his chair. The room went silent as Bill reached across to the middle of the table and took the top off the plastic Tupperware bowl, exposing Jim Mott's ashes. A voice in the crowd cut through the silence.

"Sho' ain't much left, is there?" Bill Wood looked at Luther Reynolds.

"Chief, would you do the first honors?"

Luther Reynolds stood up, picked up the spoon in front of him and dipped it into the Tupperware bowl, scooping out a heaping spoon full of Jim Mott's ashes. Luther guided the spoon slowly across the table and to the empty shotgun shell. He held the shell in a steady hand as he poured the contents of the spoon into the opened end of the red tube of the shell. All eyes in the room were wide open as they watched the ritual. There was no talk, no dogs barking, just the silence of Mott's ashes falling into the empty shell.

Spooning Ashes

Luther repeated his dip and tapped the spoon until Mott's ashes completely filled the shell. When his shell was full Luther looked around the room at the faces he knew so well.

"Jim Mott would be a friend to anybody, if they let him, and to some that didn't want to let him. His friends are rich and poor, socialite and redneck, white and black, smart and dumb as door knobs. He liked 'em all. I, for one, will miss him." A single voice came from the crowd. "Me too!"

Luther Reynolds sat down in his chair and closed the opened end of his shotgun shell, packing the ashes tight into the tube. Bill Wood looked at Dallas Thomas and nodded.

"Dallas." Dallas Thomas knew he was next to spoon out what was left of his old friend into his shotgun shell. It also took two spoonfuls to fill his shell. When it was done he looked around the room.

"I don't know how he knew all the hunters and folks in Glynn County. You can't go anywhere from Brantley Race Track to the County-Line Bar that somebody don't ask, 'How's Mott doin'?' Hell, he even knew where all the 'lost dog' pens were located from here back to Jacksonville." A single voice came out of the crowd saying, "That's the truth, now. He damn sho' did know 'em all." Dallas Thomas smiled and nodded his head. The Jim Mott ritual continued.

Leon Barrett stood near the dog pens. It was strange how so many dogs seemed to settle as the Mott ceremony began. Leon wasn't a superstitious man, but the silence was giving him an uneasy feeling. A set of headlights flashed near the front gate. He turned to see who was coming. As the lights came closer, Leon recognized the purple Pontiac GTO headed toward him. His uneasy feeling had merit because he knew he was getting ready to face unwelcome visitors, Ace and Buford, the Brinlee brothers. Leon's heart pounded in his huge chest. The lights came closer and with them came trouble.

The Brinlee boys had hunted at Roads End as guests before, but they had truly worn out their brief welcome they had been given. They were mean for meanness sake. They were rude and disrespectful to others and to nature. Whoever had been responsible for them had failed miserably and they had unleashed two true devils on the rest of the human race, or at least the folks in Glynn County. The sad thing was that they were both good looking young men; they just had ugly ways about them. Buford, the younger, was the biggest. Ace, the older, was smaller, but built like a little rock. One time Jim Mott wanted to shave their heads to see if there were any sixes on them. They were surely of the devil. The GTO stopped a few feet from where Leon was standing. Ace Brinlee, the oldest and smallest, was at the wheel as the driver's side window faced Leon. A rubber purple goat was swinging back and forth from the inside rear view mirror.

"Well, Barrett, what ya doin' out here with the dogs? Where's all the ol' timers?" Leon looked into the car. He saw a young woman next to Ace in the front seat. Brother Buford was in the back seat with another woman.

"What you boy's doin' out this way on a Friday night?" Ace smiled and stuck his head out of the window.

"Now, Barrett, you know good and well it's the night before huntin' season. We wanted to bring some life to the usual dull gathering here at Roads End." Ace reached over to the young woman sitting next to him and pulled her over to his side of the car.

"Don't ya think those ol' boys in there would like to see her dance?" The woman smiled up at Leon. Her low cut tube top took Leon's eyes away from Ace for a second. Leon looked back at Ace.

"You boys don't need to be here. There's about forty men with guns, I might add, in that room." Leon looked toward the lodge. "And, if I recall, none of those men like you two at all. Neither one of you have any redeemin' qualities whatsoever." Ace interrupted Leon.

"We got guns too." Leon shook his head.

"I tell ya what. Drive on over there and take these two dancin' young ladies, and your two guns and interrupt the funeral service honoring the final wishes of Jim Mott. Let's just see how long it takes for all four of y'all to be dead right here tonight. Nobody would ever find ya. Nobody would miss ya. Go on in, I'm sure they'll welcome your disrespect." Buford's voice came from the back seat.

"I thought Mott's funeral was last month."

"It was, but he's in there right now." The woman up front moved back to the other side of the car. "Oh God! That's awful. I ain't goin' in there, forget it." The other woman in the back seat agreed. "Me neither! Come on Ace let's go on." Ace didn't like the women talking.

"Would you two shut the hell up? I say where and when we go. If I say you go in there and dance, you dance." Leon Barrett had heard enough. He reached into the car with his two huge hands and grabbed Ace Brinlee's shirt, pulling the oldest, but smallest brother out from the opened side window of the car. It was so quick and powerful that Ace was outside the car in a matter of seconds. Leon held Ace's shirt as he slammed him into the side of the purple GTO. The young man was pinned to the car and he was nose-to-nose with Leon Barrett.

"You gonna take these two whores and that mutant brother of yours and drive right back out that gate. There ain't no reason for y'all to be here. It's just y'all bein' pure hateful and that ain't gonna happen tonight." It was easy for Leon to see his aggressive tactics had surprised and scared Ace Brinlee. Leon hadn't been paying much attention to the fact that Buford, the youngest, but biggest of the two, had gotten out of the car and had made his way to behind

Leon and the Brinlees

where Leon held Ace against the car. Leon's big forearm was pressed against Ace's throat. Buford moved from behind the car and Leon saw him with his peripheral vision. Leon pushed his arm harder against Ace's throat.

"Take another step and I'll pop his head off, like I was headin' shrimp." Buford stopped at the back of the car. He could see his brother's pain and discomfort as Leon applied more pressure to his throat. Leon never took his eyes off Ace, but he spoke to Buford.

"Now, walk back around to the other side and get your dumb ass back in that car." Buford hesitated and Leon pushed harder. Ace encouraged his brother with a painful request. "Get back in the car. He ain't foolin'." Leon smiled.

"Damn, Ace, you ain't as dumb as you look." Buford went back to the other side of the car and got back into the back seat. The two young ladies were quiet. Leon moved Ace back to the driver's side door which he opened and actually put him back into the car. Ace turned the key and started the hot rod engine. Ace's face was fire red as he glared at Leon Barrett. "We gonna see you again, Barrett." Leon smiled.

"Hell boys, y'all can see me right now. Ain't nothin' stoppin' you two from gettin' out of the car right now. Ain't it funny how the real cowards of the world will always see ya later, when they can see ya right that moment. That comment never fails to amaze me." There was a few seconds of silence as Leon stood fast, waiting for the two devil boys to jump from the GTO. Ace pushed the gear shift into reverse and the purple demon mobile backed away from where Leon was standing. As the car moved backward and turned the right passenger side faced Leon. The young lady sitting in the front seat with Ace stuck her upper body out the window and pulled down her tube top exposing her big breasts. Leon's eyes widened at the surprising display as she yelled out the window.

"I ain't no whore." Leon shook his head and talked out loud to himself, "Yeah, I can see that now from here." The back tires on the GTO dug into the dirt and gravel and kicked a cloud of dust into the air as the car seemed to explode through the main gate at Roads End. Leon turned and moved back toward the building. He passed Luther's Jeep and saw that John Wood and Bullet were both asleep on a piece of canvas.

The empty shotgun shells in front of Leonard Hooks, Big Jim Blanyer, T. Coy Nichols, Ned Smith, and C.J. Mercer had all been filled with Jim Mott's ashes. Elbert Hysler was next and then Bill Wood would be the last one to spoon out and pack down his old friend. Elbert's hand shook as he moved his first spoon full to his shell. He talked as he held the spoon over the empty shell. "I knew I'd be nervous. I don't want to spill any." The room was deathly quiet as he poured the contents of the spoon into the shell. A small amount fell onto the table, but he kept pouring until the spoon was empty. He moved the spoon back for the second load. Elbert pulled the spoon back toward him. "I can't do this. I knew I couldn't do it. I'm just too nervous. Maybe someone else can fill my shell." A deep and familiar voice cut through the room. "I'll load him up." Every head turned to the front door and the direction of the voice. Leon Barrett was standing in the door way. Bill Wood was the first to respond.

"Leon, come in. I think it would only be proper for you to be a shooter. I was hoping you would want to be with us, but I didn't want to press you to do something you didn't want to do. After spending three weeks with Jim, I thought maybe that was enough. Please come to the table." Elbert Hysler gave his seat to Leon and Leon picked up the spoon. The room went silent once more as Leon reached into his Tupperware bowl with a steady hand and scooped out another spoon full of Jim Mott. He moved the spoon to the half filled shell and completed his part of the ritual. Bill

Wood was the last one at the table who had yet to fill his shotgun shell. The room was quiet as he looked around at all the faces he knew so well. He had words to say and the men of Roads End wanted to hear them.

"I'd like to thank Jim Mott for teaching so many of our young sons how to drive that old stick shift truck of his, including my son, John." Bill Wood took his spoon, dipped out another spoonful of ashes, moved it to his empty shotgun shell and poured the ashes into the red tube. He looked up at the others and smiled.

"Somehow my son, John, shot a big hole in the floor board of Jim's truck with his shotgun. John felt bad and was scared, but Jim told him not to worry and that the hole made it easier for him to track the deer while he was driving around and that the hole would help the spilled drinks to run out onto the ground." There was laughter in the room and a lone voice yelled out, "That sounds just like Jim, don't it?"

Bill Wood dipped his second spoonful of ashes out of the Tupperware bowl and poured it into the shell. The last shell was full. Ten red shotgun shells stood at attention in a circle on the big round wooden table. Bill Wood had more to say.

"Jim passed me one morning on the Shingle Mill Road as I was perched like a eagle on the top of my old Bronco, waiting for that big one to come walking up to me. He waved as he passed by and I nodded back to him. A few minutes later he began to call my name on the radio, trying to get me to answer him. I didn't want to get down and answer because I knew it was just his foolishness. He knew how comfortable I was and he was gonna get me to come down. He kept calling so I went ahead and got down to answer him on my radio in the Bronco. I remember saying, 'Mott, this had better be important and not just chit-chat, because it ain't so easy for me to get up and down off the top of my Bronco.' He came back quickly and said, 'It might not be too important to you but it is to me. I need you to come pull me out of the ditch by the Moody Canal.' It took us both two hours to get his old truck out of that ditch." A lone voice yelled out,

"I 'member that." All eyes turned to Big John Blanyer when he joined the moment of verbal tribute.

"I never will forget that time Mott used his new CB radio and tricked Foy Peavy." Big John looked at Foy and they both smiled. That lone voice called out, "I 'member that, too." Big John continued.

"Mott got Foy on the radio and disguised his voice, pretending he was 'The Nebraska Snowman' and proceeded to tell Foy about the weather and hunting in Nebraska. Foy fell for it hook, line and sinker. He bragged later about how far his radio could reach. Foy had this long conversation with the 'Snowman' comparing the hunting and weather in Nebraska and Georgia. It took all day for Foy to realize it was just one of Mott's better moments. It was a classic." There were conversations among the men in the room as they talked about Jim Mott's joke on Foy Peavy. Lonnie Sikes' voice was the next to be heard above the others.

"When I drove that truck of mine into the big ditch off Half Moon Road, Jim worked with me for three hours before we got her out. And then in the same week I went into the bog over off All Night Road and Jim was the first one to come to my rescue again. He never let me forget that wild week. He had a few remarks about my drivin', eyesight and the amount of Ancient Age I might have had in my system." All eyes turned to Leon Barrett as his voice was next to be heard.

"I'm gonna miss taken fifty dollars from Jim each time them dogs eat some gator tail." A lone voice in the crowd yelled, "Get 'em you hairy dogs" and barked like a dog a few times. The room actually seemed to shake from the thunder of forty men laughing. A new voice cut into the laughter. It was Jim Coleman. "I gotta tell y'all. I ain't gonna miss Mott's snorin' one bit. I ain't never in my life heard nothin' like it before and I'm sure I never will again. You couldn't hear the train goin' by if Jim was snorin.'" Some of the men laughed, some agreed with a head nod and others talked about their knowledge of Jim Mott's ability to rock the foundation of the building with his notorious deviated septum. A voice in the crowd yelled, "I had to go to ear plugs, myself, and I never did sleep in the same room with him."

Raymond Lloyd, better known as "Meatpacker" stepped up to the round table. No one really knew if the nickname he was branded with came from his ability to pack in the deer meat or did it refer to the amount of meat he had "packed" between his legs. He said he preferred the latter of the two choices. All the stories about Jim Mott had brought one to Raymond's mind.

"I gotta tell y'all 'bout my favorite story 'bout Mott. I know y'all will remember, but I think it's the best." Meatpacker wasn't usually a talker so everyone got quiet so they could hear what was on his mind. "I 'bout died that Thanksgiving Day when Mott came to eat and hunt dressed in a full formal tuxedo with snake proof boots on his feet. I never will forget it." The room exploded once again with talk and laughter at Raymond's reminder. "He kept it on all day, even when he ran his dogs." A voice came from the crowd. "Cumberbun and all." The room exploded again. Meatpacker had more as he yelled above the noise. "And who the hell would name their dogs, 'Precious' and 'Fartblossom'?" The laughter continued as a single voice was heard in the back of the room. "Jim Mott would, that's who."

The purple Pontiac GTO stopped on a side dirt road about a mile away from Roads End. Ace Brinlee pounded on the steering wheel with his closed fist. "That son-of-a-bitch thinks he's bad. He ain't seen bad, yet. He ain't got no idea what bad really is." The young woman in the front seat with Ace made a mistake when she decided to share her observation of Leon Barrett.

"He looked pretty bad to me, Ace." Ace Brinlee's eyes glared in the darkness at his female companion. She didn't realize her comment was not appreciated at all. Ace had to ask her. "What did you say?" She still didn't know she had made a mistake.

"I said that big man looked pretty bad to me. I was really scared he was gonna hurt you and then the rest of us. I was scared." Ace Brinlee couldn't believe his ears. He looked into the back seat where younger brother, Buford, and his female companion sat in the dark.

"Buford, did you hear what our sweet Molly just said?" Buford's big head popped up out of the dark. Buford's hair was messed up and he had dark red lipstick all over his mouth. He was face-to-face with his older brother. "Naw man, I wasn't listenin'." Ace was disgusted with them all. "She said, she thought that asshole, Barrett, was a bad man. She was scared." Buford took a deep breath.

"He is a bad man, she's right. Hell, we was all scared, 'specially you. He could'a snapped your neck like a twig if he wanted." Buford moved back to his play toy in the darkness of the back seat. Ace looked at Molly. "I ain't scared of him. He caught me by surprise. That won't ever happen again." Molly knew not to say anything else. She finally had realized her mistake and how serious Ace was when it came to the man she had flashed her breasts at fifteen minutes before. Molly wanted to ease the tension and her fear of Ace Brinlee. She moved her sexy body next to Ace and pushed her breasts against him. "Don't be mad at me, please, Ace. I've been lookin' forward to a nice night with you. Let me help take your mind off things." Ace smiled, reached down, unbuckled his belt, unsnapped his dungarees, pulled down his zipper and exposed himself to a more than willing to please, Molly. He grabbed the back of her head and a fistful of hair and pushed her head down into his lap. Ace watched the rubber purple goat swing back and forth on the mirror as Molly began to perform one of her many specialties.

At Roads End, Bill Wood had the floor. "Before we all go out to Mott's Lounge for the final leg of this delightful journey, I would like to thank everyone of you for coming here tonight and this weekend. On behalf of Jim's family, they thank you too. We'll finish up at the Lounge and then come back here if you want and prepare for the first day of the season. If you don't plan to come back, we'll see ya when we see ya."

The ten men at the table each picked up their Jim Mott filled shotgun shell and put it back into their shirt pockets. The men in the room began to talk, move around and prepare to head to the Lounge. Leon and a group of the others left the room and went outside.

Lester Rowe, the only man in the room who took a full bottle of Wild Turkey out of the box and didn't share it, stepped up to the round table. It was obvious that the quart of Wild Turkey had taken its toll on his few senses. He held a glass half filled with the brown liquid in one hand and the empty quart bottle in his other hand. Most of the men were talking and moving around the room not paying much attention to Lester. For some reason Bill Wood and James Reynolds were watching the very drunk Lester Rowe.

Lester stared at the Tupperware bowl. He put the empty bottle he was holding on the table and then he did the same with the glass of liquor. Lester picked up one of the ritual spoons that had been left on the table. Bill Wood and James Reynolds couldn't believe their eyes when Lester Rowe stuck the spoon into the Tupperware bowl and scooped out the last spoonful of Jim Mott's ashes. Lester then turned the spoon over into the glass of whiskey and watched the ashes fall slowly and dissolve in the brown liquid. Lester looked up at a stunned Bill Wood and James Reynolds and smiled a two teeth missing smile. He picked up the glass containing the Turkey and the dissolved ashes. Dallas Thomas stepped up next to Lester, as Lester moved the glass to his lips, preparing for the drink of the century. Dallas took the glass out of Lester's shaking hand.

"Give me that, you drunk son-of-a-bitch. Jim Mott ain't gonna be no BC headache powder, if I can help it." Dallas looked at Bill and James. "And you two were gonna let him drink it. Somebody put this drunk bastard in the bed."

The two devil siblings, Ace and Buford Brinlee, had both their female companions in the dark outside the Pontiac GTO. The women were completely naked and the young men had each one bent over the hood of the purple car; one on the left side and one on the right. Ace was on the left with Molly and Buford was on the right with his friend, Lucy. The woman had their naked breasts pushed against the hood of the car as they moaned and groaned and the two savages sexually attacked them from behind. Both women were willing participants in the brutal activity and made faces at each other as the two men pumped, growled and made their own animal noises. Molly didn't like how Ace was talking during the sexual activity.

"I'm gonna mess 'im up good. He ain't that bad." Molly knew Ace was having sex with her but his mind was still on that bad man, Leon Barrett. She didn't like it one bit, but she didn't say anything to Ace. She let it go.

All the vehicles parked in the front yard of the Roads End hunting camp were either on the move or getting ready to move. Engines were revving, lights flashing and horns blowing. Bill Wood and his son, John, were sitting in Bill's white Volkswagen Beatle. The Beatle had a set of deer antlers mounted on the roof right above the front windshield. The rear air-cooled engine fired up like a heavy duty lawn mower and Bill popped the clutch as the little car jumped and headed out the main gate with the other Jeeps, trucks and a cut down skeeter. John looked out the front window of the Volkswagen with his eyes wide open and his head on a swivel. The noise, lights and all around excitement had a hold on everyone, especially a soon to be thirteen year old. Bill Wood loved the look of anticipation on John's young face. He did love looking at that boy. Bill and John both jumped in their seats when Luther Reynolds pulled up next to them in his green Jeep and hit his eighteen wheeler type air horn. After John's little heart fell out of his throat and back to its proper position, he turned and smiled at his father as the white bug kept moving. All vehicles were headed and all roads lead to Jim Mott's favorite place in the woods. They were all headed to the Lounge.

Only Don Crawford, the cook, and Lester Rowe, the drunk, remained behind at the camp. Don would prepare food for when the others returned and Lester would sleep off his indulgence of the Wild Turkey. Lester seemed to waste most of his time at Roads End sleeping off a binge or sitting at the County Line Bar. He never really did very much hunting. The others didn't mind the fact he wasn't in the woods with them. They considered it a blessing that Lester Rowe wasn't somewhere in the woods pointing a gun through bloodshot eyes filled with hard liquor. Sometimes, Lester would sign in at the lodge and within minutes leave for Brunswick. He was hunting two legged deer in the local bars. That night, however, Lester Rowe would sleep it off until the morning hours brought a new thirst to his parched lips. Even though most of the hard liquor drinking was done after the hunt, Roads End was not without those who would rather drink than hunt. Lester Rowe was just such a member.

The procession of thirty hunting vehicles made its way toward the Lounge. Luther Reynolds' green Jeep led the way for the caravan of honor as it snaked its way over the old hunter's trail leading to Jim Mott's favorite section of the woods.

The purple Pontiac GTO pulled into the main gate at Roads End. Ace turned off the headlights as he drove slowly toward the lodge building. Ace noticed something strange.

"Where the hell did they go?" There were only two trucks parked near the front of the building and one by the dog pens. Molly had her thoughts.

"Maybe they all went night huntin'." Ace wasn't concerned with her thoughts at all.

"They can't hunt 'til mornin' darlin', so please just shut the hell up and stop talkin' 'bout things you don't know." Ace reached out and squeezed Molly's face with one hand near her mouth. "That mouth of yours wasn't made for talkin'." Molly pulled her face away and looked out the passenger's side window. She didn't like what Ace said to her, but she kept her thoughts to herself. The GTO was next to the cement slab at the front door of the lodge building. Buford's head popped up from the back seat again.

"What the hell are we doin' here? Let's go to Brunswick and get out of these damn woods and away from these dogs. I hate smellin' and hearin' them dogs. I ain't lost nothin' 'round here." Ace stopped the purple car. He looked into the back seat at his younger, but bigger brother. Ace reached back and stopped the rubber purple goat from swinging.

"I wanna find out where they all went so fast and why. There's somethin' strange here tonight. I'll see who stayed behind." Buford's voice came from the back seat.

"The only strange thing here tonight is how much this shit is botherin' you. Come on, man. We got money, booze, women and you wanna keep messin' with these huntin' fools out here." Molly smiled.

"Talk to him, Buford. Talk to him." Ace reached for Molly

again. He held her upper arm in his strong hand. "You can't talk no more tonight unless I ask you a question that needs answerin.' If you open your mouth again I will take you into the woods and leave you there for the snakes. Now, that's not a threat at all, that's a promise. So try me." Ace turned back to Buford. "I'm goin' in there and see what's goin' on. I'll be right back." Buford's voice came from the back seat again as Ace opened the driver's side door. "Holler if ya need me."

Ace Brinlee stepped up onto the concrete slab and walked to the door of the building. He stopped and listened at the door for a few seconds. Buford, Molly and Lucy watched out of the car windows. Ace took a heavy fist and knocked on the door. A voice came from inside the building. "Come on in, it's open." Ace turned the door knob and pushed the door open. The voice came again. "Who's there. Come on in." Ace stepped into the front room and moved the door so he could see who was talking and inviting him in. Ace Brinlee turned in the direction of the voice and saw Don Crawford standing near the kitchen. Don's eyes widened.

"What ya doin' boy, sneakin' 'round for? You don't know how to come in when somebody says, 'come on in'?" Ace stared at Don for a second. "Now, I guess ya gonna try and scare me with that evil stare of yours. Like, maybe, I'm gettin' the evil eye from ya?" Ace looked around the room.

"Where's all the assholes, ol' man?" Ace looked back at Don.

"Just me and you left, boy. We the only assholes I see. How 'bout you?" Ace's face got more intimidating.

"Why ya wanna press ya luck with me? Your friends ain't here to come to your rescue." Don smiled.

"Rescue me? Why would I need to be rescued? You come here to hurt me, boy? What would make you come here to hurt me? I ain't never said one word to you until you walked in that door like a thief in the night. What would make you want to hurt somebody

The Cook

you don't even know?" Ace stepped toward the kitchen where Don was standing behind the counter. Only the kitchen counter separated Don Crawford and Ace Brinlee.

"Where'd everybody go, ol' man?" Don shook his head.

"Ya know, even if a man is gettin' old, he don't want to be called old. It's really a rude thing to do. I think you get pleasure in bein' rude to folks. Now that I get a closer look at you, I know who you are. You're one of those boys ain't 'spose to be comin' 'round here. Which one are you?"

"You talk to much, ol' man. You ain't answered my question yet."

"Don't plan to." Ace's face went red. He was tired of the slow talking, calm, Roads End cook.

"I'm gonna ask you one more time." Don interrupted Ace's threat.

"You mean you're gonna do somethin' to me if I don't tell you where they went? What ya gonna do to me? You ain't gonna kill me are ya, just because I didn't answer your question. Damn, that would be a hell-of-a note, now wouldn't it. Get killed 'cause ya didn't answer a question that was none of your business. Ya really gonna kill me over this?" Ace's frustration level was filling quickly.

"Shut up talkin'. You need to go talk to that bitch in my car. Y'all would be perfect for each other. I ain't said I was gonna kill nobody." Don smiled and continued his annoying word game.

"So you ain't gonna kill me. Man, that's a relief. You had me worried for a minute there." Ace was beside himself.

"I ain't gonna kill ya, but I think I'll kick your smart ass 'ol butt." Ace moved to walk around the counter where Don was standing. Ace turned at the end of the counter and found himself staring down two barrels of a twelve gauge shotgun, one barrel for each of Ace's wide opened eyes. Ace stopped and was frozen with true fear. Don's mouth went dry as he held the gun up to the young man's face. His hands were steady, his eyes were clear and his lip did not quiver. He had held a gun on someone before. He was in control.

"Now, I've let you insult me and scare me long enough." Don moved the barrels until they touched Ace's forehead. "You need to start backin' up slowly to that front door and be sure that you keep your head against those barrels. We'll walk together so we don't lose contact. If we lose contact I am gonna kill you." Ace began backing up slowly as Don moved with him. "That's it, boy. Nice and easy. We're almost to the door." Buford's voice cut into the air from outside on the concrete slab.

"Ace, you alright in there?" Ace began to tremble.

"I'm fine, don't come in." Don smiled as they continued moving to the door.

"That was good, boy. You ain't as dumb as I thought." They were at the front door. Buford's voice cut through the air again.

"Ace, you sure you're alright in there?"

"I'm fine, just stay out there, dammit." Don had his last words.

"Now boy, if you're thinkin' 'bout goin' out to that car and comin' back here with a bigger gun, or any gun at all, one of us will die this night. I hope it ain't me, but it very well could be. And you're right, I am old, but wouldn't it be sad if it was you that died, as young as you are and all." The gun barrels remained against Ace's forehead. The evil one hated it that Don was still talking. Don continued. "Now, I know this is real embarrassin' for ya, me gettin' the drop on ya like this, but ya don't have to get me back. I won't tell a soul how stupid you are. If you don't tell, I won't tell. It'll be our little secret. Please don't come back for me, young man. I have faced death before and I will probably be gone soon, but I will not die easily if it is not my proper time." Ace's eyes were wide open, angry and scared. Don wasn't finished. "Now, open the door and step on outside with your brother." Ace turned slowly away from the gun barrels and opened the door. Buford stood in the door way as Ace stepped out of the building and onto the concrete slab. Buford could see the stressful look on his older brother's face. Buford had a question that Ace didn't need to hear.

"How'd ya get those two circles on your forehead?" Ace moved past his brother and got back into the GTO. He fired up the engine as Buford got into the back seat. Both young women were quiet as Ace pushed the clutch peddle to the floor and shifted into gear. The tires of the Pontiac dug into the dirt as Ace turned the car around and headed out the main gate of Roads End.

The caravan of hunting vehicles was parked in a circle around the cross road area called the Lounge. The headlights of thirty-five vehicles illuminated the dark road crossing to the extent where it looked like it was almost daytime. The hunters and friends of Jim Mott began getting out of their trucks and Jeeps and they walked to the middle of the cross roads.

If Ace Brinlee's purple Pontiac GTO had wings it would have left the road and taken flight. In his anger, Ace had pushed the car's speedometer needle to the ninety mile an hour mark and it was still moving. The other passengers had been quiet as Ace took out his anger on the open road. With the needle moving higher, the young women in tears, Buford had to speak up.

"Ace, you're gonna kill us all if you don't slow down. I'm not sure why you're so mad, but I don't want to die just 'cause you're pissed. Now, slow down, you're scarin' the hell out of us." Ace didn't respond as the car went faster. Buford had enough. He reached out and touched Ace's shoulder. "I said, slow down. Now, stop actin' like this."

The loud GTO engine made a different sound as Ace took his foot off the gas peddle and the purple rocket began to slow down to a normal speed. The relief from fear was obvious on the women's faces as Ace slowly drove the GTO off the main road and stopped on the graveled shoulder of the road. He gripped the steering wheel and stared out of the front window. The passengers were quiet as they all stared at a frustrated Ace Brinlee.

Ace pushed the door of the car open and stepped outside. He walked a few yards away in front of the car. Buford got out of the car and joined his, more than mad, older brother. "Man, you're startin' to scare and worry me. What's wrong with you tonight?" Ace turned and looked up at his younger, but bigger brother. There was meanness and evil in his eyes.

"I hate everything about that place out there. I hate 'em all." Buford shook his head.

"This thing's got too big in your head. Hell, with 'em. You don't care 'bout huntin' anyway."

"That ain't the point, Buford. They're always laughin' at us. They made us leave. They treat us like dirt. They think they're better than us. That high and mighty Barrett and Doc Wood, and the rest of 'em. I wanna kill 'em all and feed 'em to the dogs."

"Ace, we can't kill all those men, just 'cause they don't like us. If they don't want us to hunt out there, who cares? We ain't really been huntin' much. Hell, I don't even like to hunt. We both hate campin' out. I would much rather sleep with those two in the car than that smelly, snorin', fartin' bunch out there." Ace Brinlee smiled at his brother's words. Buford could see Ace had calmed down a little. He put his arm around his older brother's shoulder. "Come on, now. Molly's waitin' to satisfy your every need and you've been treatin' her like shit all night. You gotta ease up on her or she ain't gonna be 'round next time you want her." Buford turned Ace toward the car and they began to walk back. After a few steps Ace stopped.

"Buford, that ol' man back there. He put a double barreled shotgun on my forehead and backed me out of that place. I can't let that happen. Just like I can't let Barrett push me 'round like he did. I can't live with that. I won't live with that. If you don't want to help me, that's fine, but I'm payin' 'em all back for everything." Buford took a deep breath. "You know I'll help ya, but can't we enjoy these women tonight and then we'll take care of which ever ones you want." Ace smiled up at his younger brother.

"All right." Ace nodded his head. "All right." They moved back to the car.

All of the hunters were standing in the middle of the Lounge. The ten men who had sat at the round wooden table at the lodge stood in the center with all the other members standing in a bigger circle around them. Each of the ten held a shotgun under his arm in the pointed toward the ground safety position. Dallas Thomas was in charge. He stepped into the middle of the large circle and stood as one of the chosen ten. Dallas also carried his shotgun. The crowd of forty men, plus the soon to be thirteen year old, John Wood, all were quiet as they anticipated words from Dallas Thomas.

"We have a great opportunity here tonight to do something many others will never do. We will be able to fulfill the final request of a friend. I don't think that happens very many times in our lives or the lives of others. I, for one, am more than proud to be part of this night and I'm sure you all feel the same way or you wouldn't be here. As you probably all know, Jim's request was that his ashes be spread to the four winds here at his Lounge. We decided, with permission from his family, to not only spread him around out here, but to do it like he would, with a real bang. The men began laughing and talking among themselves for a few seconds. Dallas lifted his shotgun and took the shotgun shell, he had filled with Jim Mott's ashes, out of the top pocket of his shirt. The crowd went silent again.

"As you all observed earlier, ten of us have filled our shotgun shells with Jim's ashes. Now, we will all load our guns and blow Jim's ass into the air." The friends of Jim Mott's exploded with laughter and cheers at the idea of Mott ashes being shot into the air and the sight of the ten men loading their Mott filled shotgun shells into their guns. It was a sight no one on the earth had ever witnessed before. It was a moment to remember, recall and talk about for years to come. To be part of such a spectacle in honor of a fellow friend and hunter was more than special, it was wonderfully outrageous and so was Jim Mott.

Bill Wood loaded his gun with his shell and looked around at all the faces as they waited for the fireworks display to begin. He understood what it meant to be there and be part of such an honorable ceremony. As he scanned the crowd he saw the most wonderful sight of all, as far as he was concerned. His son, John, was watching him load his gun with the sacred shell. Bill smiled and John smiled back. He did love that boy.

The crowd watched the ten men as they moved into their assigned positions. Bill Wood and James Reynolds stood side-by-side facing South. Luther Reynolds and Leonard Hooks stood together facing North. Big John Blanyer and Ned Smith faced West while T. Coy Nichols and C. J. Mercer had the East direction. Leon Barrett, who took Elbert Hysler's shell, and Dallas Thomas stood in the middle of the other eight. The crowd was silent and before Dallas could give the signal the sound of a train whistle filled the air in the distance. It was a great and welcome sound and sign. Dallas Thomas gave the commands.

"Roads End hunters, shoulder your guns." All ten shotguns moved from the safety position to the firing position at each man's shoulder. It would be a ten shotgun salute. Dallas continued with the ceremony.

"Jim Mott, this is to honor your memory and your love for Roads End. North, fire!"

Luther Reynolds and Leonard Hooks pulled the triggers of their shotguns and the explosion blew the ashes of Jim Mott into

The Four Winds

the air above the pleased and stunned spectators. There was noise in the crowd. A single voice yelled out, "Did y'all hear what Mott said?" No one answered the lone question as Dallas Thomas yelled out his next command.

"South, fire!" Bill Wood and James Reynolds pulled their two triggers and sent more of Jim Mott sailing through the air above the others. More talk and noise came from the crowd as the dust from the blast settled to the ground. A voice in the crowd hollered, "Did ya hear him?" Dallas yelled over the single voice again.

"East, fire!" T. Coy Nichols and C. J Mercer did their part and pulled their triggers and once again Jim Mott flew into the air. "West, fire!" Ned Smith and Big John Blanyer sent Jim Mott into the West side of the Lounge. The same single voice yelled again. "Oh my God, did y'all hear what Mott said that time?" The crowd went silent. Dallas Thomas had to ask the lone voice. "What did he say?" The lone voice answered instantly. "He said, 'You bastards'!" The spectators and the shooters all exploded with the loudest laughter of the night. They all knew if Jim Mott was there he would have said that very thing. It was a great moment of good feelings for everyone who was privileged to be there that night. Dallas Thomas and Leon Barrett lifted their guns to the sky. The crowd stopped laughing and talking. There was silence at the Lounge once again.

With his shotgun pressed to his shoulder and his cheek against the butt of the gun, Dallas Thomas had one more thing to say.

"Good hunting, Jim Mott." Dallas Thomas and Leon Barrett pulled the last two triggers and the last of Jim Mott covered the air above the Lounge. The unusual and bizarre ceremony to honor Jim Mott would never be mentioned by any of the men or the one boy present that night. What happened at Roads End stayed at Roads End.

Don Crawford stood at the door of the Roads End lodge as he

watched a set of headlights coming through the main gate. He reached for his shotgun just in case it was Ace Brinlee returning for more forehead rings. Don set the shotgun down against the wall when he realized the lights coming his way belonged to a truck driven by Jimmy Carter. Jimmy was coming in for the morning hunt, but he wasn't able to make it for the Jim Mott fireworks display at the Lounge. Jimmy's father, James Carter, represented the family at the ritual. The truck drove up to the concrete slab as Don Crawford stepped out of the building. Don also realized Jimmy had a passenger with him as the truck stopped. Jimmy got out of the driver's side and a young man got out of the passenger side. Don Crawford had a little joke.

"Is it the Georgia peanut man, or the great hunter, Jimmy Carter?" Jimmy smiled.

"Just the hunter, my friend, and not a great one at that. Don, how are ya?"

"I'm fine Jimmy, you?" Jimmy was standing with the young man near Don at the slab.

"I'm good." Jimmy looked at the young man.

"This is my son, Jimbo. I don't think you've been here when he was here before." Don stepped to Jimbo and stuck his hand out for a shake. Jimbo was sixteen years old and he loved being at Roads End with his father.

"Pleased to meet ya, young man. We like to see the sons of our members take an interest in the hunt." Jimbo shook hands with Don Crawford. Jimmy Carter had a question for the cook.

"I guess we're too late for the ceremony." Don nodded his head.

"They've been gone a good while. I expect 'em back and hungry any time now."

"I was hopin' to get here in time, but it just didn't work out. What ya cookin'?"

Evil Ace

The purple Pontiac GTO was pulling out of a side road near the old railroad hunter's trail. Ace had to stop the car when he saw the thirty-five hunters' vehicle caravan coming in his direction. Ace's three passengers looked up when they heard Ace's voice.

"Would y'all take a look at this? What the hell's goin' on out here?" All four pairs of eyes in the GTO were wide open as the caravan drove past them. Ace and Buford recognized many of the men sitting in the trucks and Jeeps. Luther Reynolds saw Ace Brinlee's GTO and he turned to his passenger, Dallas Thomas.

"Now there's a real big pissbird for ya. Go ahead and shoot him. Pissbirds are always in season." Dallas Thomas nodded his head.

"Nobody would care, that's for sure." Luther blasted them with his air horn. The two women screamed and the two brothers jumped when the loud noise of the horn shook the air and ground around them. Ace didn't like jumping and being scared in front of the women.

"Damn, that son-of-a-bitch. I hate 'em all. He thinks 'cause he's the law he can do what ever he wants to folks. I hate 'em all, I tell ya." Ace jumped out of the car and moved closer to the road so he could see and be seen. The next vehicle that went by was Bill Wood's white bug. Young John Wood looked out the passenger's side window and saw the hateful look on Ace Brinlee's evil face. John stared at Ace as the little car went by. Bill Wood saw Ace, too.

"Oh, Lord!" John looked at his father.

"What is it, daddy? Who is that?" The car moved away and John could not see Ace anymore.

"That's Ace Brinlee and his brother, I'm sure. They're always together. Like snakes travel in pairs. That's those boys we threw out of the camp last year. They're bad boys. I don't like seeing them out here like that. They're always up to no good." John sat back in the seat and thought about Ace Brinlee's evil eyes. The last car of the caravan went by Ace. Ace's eyes widened again when he saw Leon Barrett sitting on the passenger side of the passing truck. Ace stared at Leon. Leon smiled and looked out the front window of the truck. Ace got back into the car.

"I hate 'em all."

Don Crawford, Jimmy and Jimbo Carter stood on the concrete slab outside the lodge building watching the front yard fill with the vehicles of the returning caravan. The dogs were barking as the trucks and Jeeps pulled in, but there was not much noise from the forty hunters as they began to park and make their way to the lodge. Jimmy and Jimbo stepped off the concrete to greet the others. Don the cook went back into the building to finish setting up his buffet style food arrangement. Not all of the men who attended the unique spreading of the ashes would stay the night and hunt in the morning. Most of them would remain for the evening eat and continue the fellowship they were enjoying. Only twenty of the actual forty would spend the night and hunt through the weekend. Young John Wood jumped out of the white bug. He was glad to see Jimbo Carter. Jimbo was older, but John needed someone closer to his age to talk to. Jimbo and John walked to the dog pens. Jimmy Carter nodded to Bill Wood as Bill got out of the bug.

"Well, if it ain't the one and only, Nail-Keg Jimmy Carter. It's good to see ya, Jimmy." Jimmy Carter was an excellent carpenter and jack of all trades.

"Sorry I missed the ceremony, Bill. I was hopin' to be there." Bill smiled.

"It's good you came on in. Ya daddy was with us. He and Mott were great friends."

"Yes sir, I know. I'm glad he made it. I know it meant a lot to him." Jimmy looked at Jimbo and John as they walked toward the dog pens. "John's gettin' big, huh?" John was Bill's favorite subject.

"He'll be a teenager after midnight tonight. And look at Little

Nail, Jimbo. It seems like just yesterday and he was gonna be a teenager. He looks more like a man every time I see him." Jimmy smiled.

"He's sixteen already. Hard to believe, ain't it?" Jimmy liked looking at his son, Jimbo, as much as Bill liked looking at his son, John. Daddies are supposed to like looking at their sons. Bill and Jimmy walked toward the concrete slab. Luther Reynolds walked up behind them.

"Did y'all see that ugly pissbird standin' on the road out there?" Bill knew who Luther was referring to.

"Yes sir, Chief. I always get a bad feeling whenever the Brinlee boys are within a hundred miles from here." A familiar voice cut through the night. Leon Barrett stepped into the light on the concrete slab.

"Those two devils were in the yard earlier. They had two pretty little whores with 'em. They wanted to come in and disturb our little get together. I roughed 'em up a little and ran 'em off." Bill Wood was concerned.

"Be careful with those two, Leon. I know you can take care of yourself, but they're mean and sneaky. They wouldn't face ya straight up. It would come from behind. Cowards work like that. Just be careful." Leon smiled and moved to the front door.

"I'm hungry." Chief Luther Reynolds turned to the front gate as the others walked into the building. He shook his head as he saw the purple Pontiac GTO fly past the gate and disappear into the darkness. He followed the others into the lodge.

Don Crawford was all smiles as he watched his friends and fellow hunters lined up, plates in hand, at the buffet styled dinner he had prepared. The true cooks of the world always love to see people eat. After dinner, twenty of the men would leave because they had only come to honor Jim Mott and participate in the spreading of the ashes ritual. The twenty men who remained after dinner would divide up into different groups. A number of the elders would circle up at the big wooden table and the playing cards would fly around the wooden poker table. Some of the other men would sit outside near the camp fire and talk about their dogs, hunting moments of the past and the hunt facing them come morning. A few of the younger and single hunters would go into Brunswick, or to the County Line Bar or perhaps even a run out to the Darien Truck Stop where the ladies of the Georgia evening had set up shop.

John Wood and Jimbo Carter walked into the lodge building to join the men for a spot in the buffet line. It took Jimbo only a few seconds to realize he should have eaten later, when the men had gone about their other business. His stomach turned sour and his heart raced like that GTO engine when he heard that awful, embarrassing question that had been asked for years of the young men of Roads End. A single voice from the crowd in the room took Jimbo's appetite.

"Hey, Little Nail, you got any pussy, yet?" The room exploded with laughter from the unfeeling adult hunters. Jimbo's eyes popped open and his handsome young face went blood red. It is never any fun when the wild laughter in the room is at your expense. The laughter faded and that single voice didn't let up on the embarrassed young hunter. "Well, have ya?" The crowd of fun loving, but very insensitive men were quiet in anticipation of Jimbo's reply. The single voice added to Jimbo's awkward and humiliating moment. "Are ya still able to keep your hands warm by rubbing that little pecker of yours." Jimbo could not stay in the room and endure more sexual interrogation. He turned and was out the door as the laughter continued. John Wood smiled at his father and picked up a plate for his food. Bill Wood knew it wouldn't be long and John would face those same questions. He knew they would both have to face that Roads End traditional dilemma when it came about. Jimbo stood outside the building. He had forgotten about the trick that had been played on him when he was eight years old. He couldn't believe that single voice had reminded him and everyone else in the room about that mean, but funny trick.

Jimbo was in the third grade and his father had brought him for a weekend of hunting. At one time during the day, while in the woods, Jimbo had complained about his hands being so cold. His uncle and another hunter took that opportunity to introduce the eight year old to an interesting male encounter. They told Jimbo if he would grab hold of his, far from manly, little wacker and rub it up and down, his hands and the rest of his body would stay warm. The story went that Jimbo tried this method quite often after his introduction, even to the extent that he showed his teacher at the elementary school and a few classmates how to keep warm on a cold day on the school playground. It was his parents first visit to the school for disciplinary actions for Jimbo. Jimmy Carter took a plate of food outside to his red-faced son. Jimbo was near the dog pens.

"You all right, boy?" Jimbo smiled.

"Yes sir, I should'a known that was comin'. He did that to me last time. I ain't mad, I just don't know what to say." Jimmy Carter touched his son on his head.

"Remember, you don't owe nobody no answer. You'll have an answer for him one day, but you don't have to answer if you don't want to. A good answer when somebody wants to know about you and a woman is, 'That ain't none of your business'. Real men don't talk about women like that. If a woman thinks enough of you to be with you in that way, be respectful and keep that secret to yourself. You'll be a better man 'cause ya did."

Jimmy Carter left his son with the plate of food, the dogs barking and wonderful words of manly wisdom. If it wasn't for that night at Roads End and that awful question, Jimmy would have never been given the opportunity to share his philosophy on how to treat a woman with his son. If Jimmy Carter and his son, Jimbo, didn't kill a deer that weekend it was already worth the long ride to Roads End.

Jimmy walked to the door of the lodge building as a few of the others were coming out of the door. The group of hunters who were not staying through the weekend began to say good night, start their vehicles and head home. The group of men thinned out and only twenty hunters and two young men remained. Jimbo ate his food while he watched the trucks and Jeeps leaving and disappearing into the dark. John Wood walked out of the building and joined Jimbo at the dog pens. John just wanted to be with his friend. He didn't mention or even care about the embarrassing moment Jimbo had endured earlier.

"Y'all always have the most dogs out here, don't ya?" Jimbo's eyes and face lit up when he looked at their pen filled with thirty hunting dogs.

"I think I like runnin' the dogs more than I like huntin'." John could tell Jimbo liked talking about the dogs. He listened to his friend continue. "My Uncle Donny sure loves to make a drive with these dogs. He taught me 'bout road huntin' and still huntin', but I know his favorite is runnin' the dogs. Mine, too. I love to hear those dogs when they make that drive in the woods and they jump that deer and run him out of the block." John's eyes and ears were both wide open as the sixteen year old hunter shared his heart and feelings about hunting at Roads End.

A few of the men who were staying the weekend were still eating inside the building while six of the elders had taken their places at the poker table. Straight up seven card stud would be the only game for the first few hours of dealing the cards.

Dallas Thomas sat with Lonnie Sikes on one side of the table. Bill Wood and James Reynolds were on the other side of the table with Big John Blanyer at one end and Jacksonville Police Chief Luther Reynolds perched at the other end. Leonard Hooks, Ned Smith and C. J. Mercer were sitting in chairs near the table as spectators for the time being. They would not play for now, but would join the game later as others lost, got tired or just wanted to give up their seat. Bill Wood was the first dealer of the night and had just dealt three down cards to the five other players and to himself.

"Seven card stud, gentlemen. Roll your own."

Clayton McKendree, Scott Milligan and Bruce Couey walked past the poker table on their way to the front door. Chief Luther Reynolds took a deep breath and made an observation. "Holy shit, boys. You pissbirds smell like French whores. What the hell is that. It sure ain't Old Spice, I'll tell ya that." Clayton smiled at the old man's funny question.

"I don't know 'bout these other two, but I'm wearin' Jade East, Mr. Luther. It attracts the best women and it drives 'em wild, sir." Chief Reynolds shook his head.

"Well, well, would you look at Hollywood here. If he ain't dressed to kill and smellin' like he's already dead. That smell ain't gonna attract nothin' but green butt blow flies. Unless you're plannin' on goin' to China tonight, count on bein' alone." The poker game stopped as Luther Reynolds tried to help the young men with a suggestion and offer. "I think there's a bottle of Old Spice in the john. You're all welcome to splash a little on so you can get the real women to notice ya." Clayton, Scott and Bruce were at the door hoping to get away before any more conversation with the old timer had to be endured. They respected the old gentleman, but his bottle of Old Spice would not be pulled from its resting place unless Luther splashed it on himself. Bill Wood had a fatherly warning for the young men.

"You boys know we would never tell y'all what to do, but please be careful if y'all go over to that truck stop. There's some bad people over that way." Clayton smiled. He respected and appreciated Bill's honest concern.

"We were gonna go into Brunswick and find some dancin' girls." Chief Reynolds had to share more of his experienced thoughts.

"There's two kind of dancin' girls, fellas. The ones who dance with you, like the ones at the VFW and the ones who will dance for ya, when all you have to do is sit there and watch. I prefer watchin' 'em, myself." The men within range of Luther's voice exploded with laughter. The three young men took that opportunity to get out the door. Dallas Thomas made the first bet of the night. "I'd be goin' against nature if I didn't bet the five dollar limit on that pair of hooks.

Jimmy Carter stood at his dog pen looking at his thirty dogs with his son, Jimbo, and John Wood. They watched Bruce Couey and the other two young men drive off through the main gate. They were headed into town in search of the dancing ladies of Brunswick, Georgia. As the truck disappeared into the darkness the lights of another truck came through the front gate.

Jimmy and the two young men watched the truck as it rolled right up to them at the dog pens. The truck stopped and Tom McGehee, another hunter and friend, stepped out of the driver's side. His fifteen year old son, Tom Jr., although they called him, Little Mac, stepped out of the passenger's side. Jimmy greeted his friend and fellow hunter.

"Well, we didn't think you were comin' this week." Mac stuck out his hand to Jimmy as he moved toward him.

"I didn't think so either, but here we are. How ya doin' Jimmy?"

"I'm good. You know my boy, Jimbo, and that there is Bill Wood's boy, John." Mac nodded and smiled at the two young men.

"Y'all remember my boy, Little Mac, don't ya? He was hopin'

y'all would be here." Both John and Jimbo liked to see another hunter closer to their age.

At the poker table, inside the lodge building, the old pissbird, himself was raking in the first hand of a long poker night. He puffed on his cigar and cradled the money as he pulled it toward him from the middle of the big table. Big John Blanyer had to comment on the first hand.

"I had to stay. You can't fold with a full boat no matter how little it is. I had to see it. Damn, Chief, a queens over jacks boat on the first hand, what a great hand to start the night with." Chief Reynolds nodded, gave a big grin, and gave his early win philosophy.

"You know I hate winning that first hand, 'cause your expectations get so high for the rest of the evening. You know this money's gonna change locations a lot of times before it settles with one winner. I think winning early is a bad omen." Bill Wood smiled and made his own observation.

"Yeah, we all noticed how much you hated pullin' all that money to your side of the table. It sure don't look like any bad omen to me." The players and spectators laughed as Luther gave that big grin again. It was the winner's turn to deal. Luther handed the shuffled deck to Bill Wood for the cut. Bill tapped the cards to let them ride as they were. Luther picked up the deck. "Ante up a dollar, gentlemen." They all tossed a dollar to the middle of the table. Luther dropped the first card in front of James Reynolds and made his call, "Same game, same winner." The Roads End traditional poker game continued.

Jimmy Carter and Tom McGehee walked into the front door of the lodge building leaving the three young boys at the dog pens. The new arrival, Little Mac, had an idea.

"I been thinkin' 'bout the last time we were here and how wild it was when we layed near the train tracks when the train went by. I haven't been able to stop thinkin' 'bout that night. It was wild."

He looked at Jimbo. "Jimbo you were there, wasn't it crazy?" Jimbo remembered and nodded.

"It was crazy all right. And scary, too." John's eyes were wide open as the older two boys continued. "We've been here for awhile now and I ain't heard a train whistle yet. John's been here all day." Jimbo looked at John. "John, you heard the whistle today?"

"Just earlier today, but nothin' tonight. I hadn't thought about it, but nothin' tonight, so far." Little Mac's eyes lit up. "Then she's due." Jimbo and John were both ready for some excitement and Little Mac's suggestion was just the ticket they needed. John had not been with the boys on their train adventure the year before, but he would be thirteen in a few hours and it was time for him to join the other teenagers and what ever that meant. The three boys walked away from the dog pens and walked out of the main gate. They didn't realize they were not just leaving, but they were leaving the safety of Roads End. Young people never think about the safe atmosphere that may surround them. It is easy to take such things for granted. The three young men became train hunters in a matter of seconds.

Leon Barrett and Raymond "Meatpacker" Lloyd walked by the poker table as Chief Luther Reynolds was raking in his second win in a row off the table. The table was quiet as the money moved in the same direction as before. Leon interrupted the player's thoughts. "Me and Packer are headed to town. We'll keep an eye on those Jade East boys if we can find 'em." Bill Wood smiled.

"And who's gonna keep an eye on you two?" Leon smiled back at Bill.

"Don't wait up for me, daddy." They all laughed as Leon and Raymond walked out the door. Chief Reynolds had a suggestion.

"We gonna talk all night or play cards? Let's play. Who's deal is it?" The five other players all responded at the same time. "Shut the hell up!" They all roared with laughter including the big winner at the moment.

The cold night air had moved in as the three young train hunters walked along the Seaboard Coast Line railroad tracks. Jimbo had made the statement that it was scary out there the year before, but he would show no fear that night. They had walked about a quarter mile to a signal light tower next to the tracks. As they approached the tower all six eyes widened and three hearts began to pound when the whistle from a train blew in the distance. Little Mac was right, she was due. They all looked in the direction of the sound.

The old pissbird himself had won three of the first hands at the poker table and he had folded early in the one game he lost, not contributing much of his own money to the pot at all. His seat was a hot one and he had fallen into the old poker adage, "Everything's funny when you got plenty of money." Luther was way too happy as he waited for the next hand to be dealt. The others didn't want to look at Luther's Cheshire cat smile. It was Bill Wood's turn to deal. "Same game, different winner."

Three young hearts pounded in three young chests when the train whistle sounded again and they could see the light on the front of the engine about a mile away as it made the curve near White Oak Swamp. Little Mac knew the reason he was there.

"Come on y'all. Let's lay down on the ground by the tower. It's a crazy feelin' when the ground starts shakin' around you as it goes by." Jimbo knew what Little Mac was referring to. John had no idea at all what was going to happen, but he was locked into what ever being a true teenager meant at that moment. The light on the train was about a half mile away.

Little Mac took his position on the ground next to the light tower. He lay on his stomach facing the oncoming train. His body was about three feet from the track. Jimbo did the same with his head about two feet from the bottom of Little Mac's boots. John was still standing as the older two boys lay flat on their stomachs.

Daredevils

Neither of the older boys paid any attention to John as he did not hesitate to join them as the third member of the face down on your belly train hunters.

The huge engine of the first train of the night was only a few hundred yards away and moving fast. All three boys could feel the ground tremble around them. Everything started shaking and their young bodies bounced and pounded the ground. Their three heads were lifted and looking at the train at first. Their eyes widened as the train came closer and the noise became louder. John dropped his head as the train flew past them. The ground was trembling under the three daredevils. Little Mac kept his head up and yelled as the freight cars rolled by. He didn't yell anything in particular. It was just a wild rebel yell to add to the wild and dangerous moment.

Jimbo looked back at John to see if he was still there. John peeked up over his arms and forced a brave smile at Jimbo. The caboose went flying by. Little Mac jumped to his feet.

"Oh man! I've been waiting to feel that again. Oh man! That was great! Oh man!" Little Mac couldn't contain himself. He danced around in his long awaited moment of excitement. Jimbo helped a shaken John Wood to his feet.

"You all right?" John nodded with a wide-eyed look. "Ya did good." John smiled, but still had no words. John would keep their secret and burn it deep into his belly. He was very close to being thirteen as he took a step toward manhood. The boys began walking back to Roads End. Little Mac was beside himself. "Oh man!"

The three night time train daredevils began walking back to the safety of the lodge and the dog pens. Little Mac was leading the way with John and Jimbo side-by-side behind him. Little Mac heard the music first and stopped, holding his hand out as a signal so the others would stop and listen.

"Listen, y'all." They all stopped. John and Jimbo heard it too.

They all three recognized the sound of the tune, "Satisfaction" by the Rolling Stones. It was an unusual sound to be coming from the woods ahead of them. The three adventurers were next to each other and no one was the leader. Little Mac whispered to his two friends.

"Somebody's out here with a radio." John didn't like the situation. He was scared.

"Who?" John looked at Little Mac then at Jimbo. "Who would be playin' a radio out here?" Jimbo, the oldest, had the answer.

"Somebody's makin' out. They're parkin' out here. We need to go on back and leave them alone." Little Mac's eyes lit up.

"I wanna see 'em. Let's just get a little closer and take a look. We can run if we have to." Jimbo knew better.

"Folks don't like it when they get disturbed in the woods. 'Specially if they're "doin' it." John's eyes lit up along with Little Mac's. He was more determined, now.

"I'm goin' in closer. I hope they are doin' it." Little Mac walked into the woods in the direction of the music. Jimbo didn't want to follow, but he would not leave his friend. John didn't move until Jimbo followed Little Mac, but he liked the possibility of seeing someone "doin' it." John followed Jimbo into the thick woods.

The music got louder as they moved slowly and they could see a set of car headlights through the trees and bushes. Little Mac dropped down low to the ground and was on all fours as he moved slowly, then quickly toward the lights. John and Jimbo followed his lead and they were all crawling on the ground in a matter of seconds. Little Mac stopped as the other two moved next to him, one on each side. Six young eyes popped open to their fullest ever when they saw two young women, wearing only their panties, dancing to the music in front of the car lights. Two men were sitting on the hood of the car watching the women dance. Both men turned liquor bottles up to their lips as the women danced up to them.

The Dancers

The three young peeping spectators were mesmerized by the incredible sight they were beholding in the deep woods near Roads End. Little Mac and Jimbo had no idea they were watching Lucy and Molly dance for the Brinlee brothers, Ace and Buford. But, John had seen Ace Brinlee earlier that night standing on the side of the old hunter's trail as the caravan was headed back to the lodge. John didn't realize it was Ace until he slid off the hood of the purple GTO and walked in front of the car lights, grabbing one of the women as she danced. Ace handed her his bottle and as the woman turned it up to her lips, Ace grabbed and squeezed one of her breasts. He then took the bottle from her and pushed her over the hood of the car. He then buried his head against her bare breasts. The six young eyes took in every movement. John wanted to see more, but he also wanted to tell the others what he knew. John turned to Little Mac.

"That's Ace Brinlee and his brother. My dad says they're bad men."

Little Mac and Jimbo both looked at John and then they looked back at the lights. As the three young men watched the women dancing in front of the lights, Jimbo was the first to notice something was different. He didn't see Ace or Buford Brinlee. Jimbo turned his head toward Little Mac and he had a question.

"Where did the brothers go? I don't see 'em, do you?" John looked across Little Mac to Jimbo. His eyes were wide open with pure fear as a new and strange voice coming from behind them changed the blood flow in John's thirteen year old veins.

"Gettin' a good look, boys?" All three young men turned to see the evil Ace and Buford Brinlee standing over them. John was instantly sick to his stomach. He had never been so scared. The two older boys were frozen with their own fear as the brothers looked like giants standing over the three daredevils. Ace's voice added to their already visible fear.

"You little sneaky bastards get your little rocks off crawlin' 'round in the woods watchin' folks?" None of the boys made a move. "Me and Buford ought'a kick y'all's little peepin' tom asses." Ace reached down and grabbed John, the smallest, by his belt and pulled him up off the ground like he was a rag doll. John made a noise of fear as the air was forced out of his lungs when his belt pressed against his stomach. His little gasping moan of fear, pain and desperation was just enough to send Jimbo and Little Mac into a fifth gear panic mode. Both of the oldest boys exploded off the ground and it was every man, or better still, every boy, for himself. Little Mac and Jimbo ran in different directions leaving John with the two bad brothers.

John's head was on a swivel as he looked one way to see Little Mac disappear into the dark woods to his left and then a turn of his head helped him see Jimbo do the same disappearing act to his right. John Wood would be thirteen years old in a little over an hour, but at that moment he didn't feel very confident he would ever celebrate that happy occasion. He was alone in the dark woods with naked women dancing to Mick Jagger and a Brinlee brother standing on each side of him. Ace's voice changed and curdled John's blood flow once again.

"Damn boy, did your friends haul ass or what? I ain't never seen nobody move like that." Ace looked at Buford. "You ever seen that before, Buford?" Buford shook his head, but didn't talk. Ace had a question for his younger, bigger and quieter brother. "Buford, how far is it to that water hole where Hamp put them four big gators last week? Them damn Florida bull gators love eatin' at night and we just might have some good gator bait right here with this little shit." Buford had his first answer of the conversation. "It ain't but a half mile from here." The music stopped and Molly's voice cut into the night.

"Ace, what y'all doin' in there? Get out of the dark and come back here in the light. We're scared out here without y'all. Ace, it's cold. Are you in there?" Ace pressed his lips together and took a deep breath. "Will you shut the hell up. And put some clothes on. Both of ya." Ace was almost nose-to-nose with his frightened prey. Ace was at his meanest when he had a scared victim. The true cowards of the world can only intimidate the weak. "What's ya name, boy?" John's mouth was dry and he could feel his heart pounding in his chest. "You ain't deaf or nothin' are ya, boy?" John took a deep breath.

"No, sir." Ace smiled and looked at Buford.

"Damn, this gator bait's got manners." Ace grabbed the front of John's coat and pulled the scared boy closer than he had been to the evil one, up to that moment.

"I asked you what your name was and I don't think you answered me. I don't think I like that. I think that's real disrespectful." John was far too scared to answer the question. He only stared at his tormentor. Buford had an observation.

"Can't you see this boy's almost scared to death. Turn him loose and let's get out of here." Ace heard Buford's words, but didn't take his eyes off his young scared victim.

"He ain't goin' nowhere 'til he tells me his name." John realized his words could possibly bring his freedom and continued life. He looked at Ace Brinlee.

"John. I'm John Wood." Ace's eyes lit up.

"You ain't Doc Wood's boy, are ya?"

"Yes sir." Ace smiled a real evil one.

"Well, well. Buford, did you hear that? This here little peepin' tom ain't none other than Bronco Bill Wood's scared little boy." Buford didn't like what he had just heard.

"We need to get on out of here, Ace. Let the boy go on. We've scared him enough. And besides, we don't need Doc Wood and the rest of them crazy hunters huntin' for us in the dark over this little rack of bones." Buford looked at John. Ace did not agree with his younger, but bigger brother. "I ain't scared of nobody in that camp." Buford shook his head.

"Nobody said you was scared. I just think it's time to go on home and take them two beauties with us. Ain't ya scared him enough for one night? Hell, his jackrabbit friends are probably tellin' the others he's here right now. I ain't too crazy about facin' all those guns over this foolishness." Molly blew the horn of the purple Pontiac GTO.

"Ace, y'all come on, please. It's gettin' cold and we're tired. Let's go, please." Ace grabbed the front of John's coat again and pulled John toward him. He had to scare the young man one more time. "Tell that daddy of yours he ought'a keep you out of these woods at night. And tell him if I catch you lookin' at my woman again, like a sneaky little pervert, I'm gonna fix ya like they fix them dogs sometimes and then feed ya to them gators." Ace pushed John away and let go of his coat. "Now git, before I change my mind." Ace didn't have to repeat his command. John turned and like his two older friends, he disappeared into the dark woods. John was at his fastest running speed in a matter of seconds. He didn't know where he was headed, but that really didn't matter at that particular moment.

Jimbo and Little Mac ran threw the front gate of Roads End and both boys had to jump to the side as a set of headlights were headed in their direction. A truck horn sounded and the truck stopped a few feet from the boys. They were both standing at the passenger's side window. Leon Barrett stuck his head out the window.

"What the hell you two doin' out here in the dark like this? We could'a ran you over and not even known it 'til the buzzards showed up in the mornin'." Both boys were out of breath from their run, but Jimbo found the strength to talk, as he panted.

"It's John. They got John." Leon opened the door of the truck and stepped to the ground with the boys.

"Who's got John? What happened?" Little Mac took a deep breath.

"The Brinlee brothers got him. We ran, but John didn't get away." Leon looked into the truck at Meatpacker.

"Let's go find the boy. Those stupid fools ain't crazy enough to hurt him, but I'll bet they're scarin' the shit out of him right now." Leon looked at Jimbo and Little Mac. "Get in the truck and tell Meatpacker where to go. I'll be in the back." The two boys climbed into the cab of the truck as Leon jumped into the back. Meatpacker hit the gas and they were out the gate with a dust trail smoking behind them. Leon Barrett stood up looking over the top of the cab with both his hands on the top.

The biggest pot of the night was piled up in the middle of the big round wooden table. Bill Wood, Luther Reynolds, James Reynolds and Dallas Thomas were all still in the seven card stud game. Chief Reynolds was having the best night at the table of anyone in the history of Roads End poker. His winnings were substantial and it was still rather early as "card time" usually went. There was easily, seven hundred dollars waiting to be won and dragged from the center of that big table. Each remaining player had a hand in front of him good enough to win most pots, but only one had the hand for that one. They all had to stay in the game with what they were holding. There was too much at stake, not to see their hand to the end.

Bill Wood had his best hand of the night. He tried not to show his excitement as he worked to keep his cool poker face. He looked down at his cards and saw what the others saw; two jacks and one queen showing in the four visible cards. What the others didn't know was another queen and a third jack were hidden in the three down cards. Bill's confidence was as high as it had been so far that night. He knew a jacks over queens full house would be hard to beat and such a hand would be a true confidence builder for any gambling man.

James Reynolds looked around the table and was bathing in his own moment of confidence. From what he could see he was about to win the big one. He had an ace and a pair of sevens showing and he knew he had two more aces hidden on the down side. James knew it would be a shock to the other three when he turned those two aces over and took the big pot with his own full house. He couldn't wait to be the spoiler and he was ready to bet the farm as soon as the last bet came from Luther. He knew his full boat would take Bill Wood to the cleaners.

Dallas Thomas had the weakest hand on the table. He just didn't know it, yet. The possibility he had the heart flush was pretty obvious with four hearts showing. It was a good bet he had one more underneath in the three down cards. He knew he had to stay in the game, because a flush is usually hard to beat in most games, but not that game.

It was Luther Reynolds' turn to bet, check or fold and they all were waiting for his decision. Luther looked around the table as if he were a Gypsy fortune teller and he was reading everybody's cards one more time. Everyone had seven cards so the deal was over and it was time for the final round of bets to be cast into the already huge pile of money in the middle of the table.

After Luther made his last scan of the cards he looked down at his own hand. He had a two, three, six of clubs and a ten of spades showing. He lifted two of his down cards and took another peek. He didn't look at the other down card. He knew he wouldn't be needing it. An impatient-to-win Bill Wood reminded the Chief it was his turn to bet.

"You bettin' or checkin', Chief?" Luther didn't look up.

"Well boys, I tell ya what. Dallas, you're suckin' hind tit with that little chickenshit flush of yours. You might as well save your money for the next game. You already put enough in that pot. You addin' more to it will just be pure ridiculous on your part, but do what's best for you, don't let me influence you in any way." Dallas gave a little grin, and he knew Luther was probably right, but he hated to drop out, just in case. He would never forgive himself if he let Luther talk him out of the winner. Luther had more.

"And you other two high rollers ain't had shit all night and now one of 'em's most likely got that boat he's been waitin' for all night. Hell, maybe both of 'em's got a boat. Damn, I hate to take a hand like this away from the cards you boys are holdin'. It just don't seem right. Me winnin' this pot will probably break up the game, but I'm sure havin' fun with you boys. I'd hate to see it end." Bill Wood couldn't take any more.

"Chief, make your bet or check to James." Luther smiled.

"Save your money, boys. Think hard before you call me on this one. I feel like y'all's daddy tryin' to give you some good advice. This is my hand and I'm tryin' to save y'all some money so we can keep playin'. " Luther picked up some money from the stack of bills in front of him. "I bet a hundred dollars." All eyes around and away from the table popped open. If everyone called his bet there would be over a thousand dollars in the middle of the table. James Reynolds put his hand on the money in front of him and thumbed through it to see if he could cover the bet without digging into his wallet. Luther had another warning.

"Save it, son. You can't beat me." Bill Wood had to speak up.

"Chief, nobody's gonna fold in this game because you tell 'em to. You can't run us out of this one." Bill looked at Luther's cards. "Besides the odds of you havin' the four and five of clubs hidden in your hand is more ridiculous than that hundred dollar bet you just made to scare us off. There is no way on Earth you are sitting there with a club straight flush. I don't think we've ever even seen one at this table in the years we've been playin'. And I, for one, don't think we'll see one tonight. So, if these two will bet or fold, I'm gonna bump your ass right off the table when the bet gets to me. So get ready 'cause I'm with you 'til the end."

James Reynolds threw his money into the pot and called Luther's bet. He had two twenties left in front of him. Dallas Thomas surprised Bill Wood and threw his flush into the middle of the table and reluctantly folded, what was usually considered a good hand. Bill's theory of nobody folding went out the window as Dallas' cards slid into the pile of money and Dallas sat back in his chair to become a spectator. Bill Wood was true to his word. He threw his money into the pot.

"Here's your hundred and I'll raise you another hundred." Luther didn't hesitate.

"Damn, Bill! Here's your hundred." Luther threw the money on the table and looked at Bill. "Is there another raise left?" Dallas, the spectator, knew the answer.

"One more, Chief." They always played the house rule of a three raise limit. Luther smiled. "And I'll raise you another hundred." James Reynolds hesitated and Luther made the wildest play of the night.

Luther picked up two of his down cards licked the back of them both and slapped them against his forehead, making the two cards stick to his skin with the face of the cards out so everyone could see them. Luther moved his head to the right and then to the left so the cards could be seen by all who wanted to see them. He stopped moving his head and looked right into Bill Wood's wide opened eyes, revealing the fact that he did have the two cards needed for a straight flush and the winning hand.

"Bet if ya feel froggy, son."

Bill Wood and James Reynolds were both in poker shock. The fact that Luther was kind enough to reveal his hand before he took

The Hand

all their money made no difference to the two full house holders. It was adding more salt to the wounds to see those two cards stuck to his head than it would have been to see him turn them over after they had bet all their money. The spectators exploded with laughter. Dallas Thomas shook his head and laughed too. There were no smiles on the faces of the two beaten players. No laughter coming from them at all, as they watched the old pissbird himself pull that huge pile of money toward his belly. It was a once in a lifetime hand and it had come at the right moment for Luther Reynolds. And the Chief was right about his prediction. It broke the game up for the night. The others would not be able to recover mentally until a later time, perhaps the next night.

Meatpacker had his truck wide open on the hunters trail dirt road. His two passengers had directed him to the open area near the railroad tracks where they had left John Wood to the no mercy Brinlee siblings. Leon Barrett remained at his observation post standing in the back of the truck. He took a deep breath of the cold November air as the lights of the truck cleared the way through the darkness.

Ace Brinlee stood about ten yards away from his Pontiac GTO like he was standing guard. His brother, Buford, was in the warm back seat of the car with his woman, Lucy, wrapped around him like adhesive tape. Molly was squatting behind a bush near Ace.

"Ace, don't let anybody see me. I'm embarrassed. Damn, it's cold." Ace turned to the speaking bush.

"Are you crazy? Who the hell's gonna see you in the dark over there? Buford and Lucy's in the damn car. I got my back turned and unless that little shit peepin' tom has come back, ain't nobody within miles of here. Nobody would even know you're back there if they did come by. And you been dancin' 'round here naked all night and now you're cold. You are somethin' else, woman. Hurry up and let's get out of here." The bush talked again.

"I'm tryin' to hurry, but I'm nervous." Ace turned toward the woods behind Molly when he saw lights and heard the roar of a truck engine. The lights were moving straight toward Molly and the talking bush. She screamed when the truck lights flashed in her face and lit up her hiding place. Molly was still screaming as Ace jumped away from the squatter's hiding place and left her to her fate with the moving truck. Meatpacker and the two boys saw Molly's naked body dive from behind the bush and out of harm's way. Leon saw her too, but he also saw Ace Brinlee running toward the open ditch next to the dirt road. Leon picked up Meatpacker's ax handle off of the bed in the back of the truck. Meatpacker turned the bouncing truck toward Ace and it was next to the fleeing coward in a matter of seconds.

Ace looked back as the truck pulled up next to him. He only saw the front of the truck as he ran beside the deep, water filled ditch. There was fear in Ace's eyes as the side of the truck pushed him closer to the ditch. Ace would have been even more scared if he had seen Leon Barrett swing the ax handle, hitting Ace between his shoulder blades, taking him off his feet and sending him airborne into the cold water of the deep drainage ditch.

The two boys couldn't believe their eyes when Ace went flying into the ditch and Meatpacker turned the truck around and headed for the GTO. The boys could see Buford Brinlee jumping out of the back seat of the car as the truck slid up near the car. Leon Barrett jumped out of the truck bed and he slammed into the younger, but bigger Buford Brinlee. With his best football coach's technique, Leon buried his shoulder into the chest of Buford Brinlee in a classic open field tackle and took him off his feet and to the ground in one continuous motion. The air in Buford's lungs exploded out of his body as he hit the ground with Leon's shoulder still pressed against his sternum. Leon knew he had hurt the big boy. He knew the sound of pain. Leon stood over the helpless and gasping for air, Buford Brinlee.

"Don't get up, boy. Just stay down. I know it hurts, but you'll get your air back in a little while. You ain't gonna die." Buford looked up at Leon with a painful grimace that asked the question, "Are you sure I'm not dying?" Leon had his own question.

"Where's the boy? I'm only gonna ask you one time." Buford knew he had to find the air to talk or more pain was coming. He spoke with a painful whine in his voice.

"We let him go 'bout half hour ago. We didn't hurt 'em at all. Just tried to scare him 'cause he and those other boys were hidin' in the woods watchin' us. You'd a done the same thing, Leon." Meatpacker stepped up next to Leon.

"Let's go back. John might be back at the lodge. Maybe we'll find him on the way back. These boys ain't worth all this. Come on." Leon knew Meatpacker was right. The two big men left Buford on the ground and got back into the truck. Leon went to the passenger's side and made the two boys get into the back of the truck for the cold ride back to Roads End. As the truck moved away, Molly stepped out of the woods and into the lights of the truck. Meatpacker stopped the truck to get a good look at the full bodied and naked Molly. With no clothes and no shame, she stood at Leon's window. All the eyes in the truck looked at her every curve. Leon couldn't help himself.

"You are too pretty, ma'am, to be out in the woods like this with these cowards. Good night." Meatpacker hit the gas and the truck disappeared into the woods. Lucy brought a coat to Molly and she wrapped her cold, naked and trembling body in it quickly.

As the women moved back to the car, Buford was on his feet, but it was obvious he was still hurt. A wet and muddy Ace Brinlee staggered up behind the car and fell across the top of the trunk. Buford moved slowly to help his older, but smaller brother. Molly and Lucy stood next to the trunk of the car. Ace looked up at his brother.

"What the hell happened?" Molly didn't give Buford the opportunity to answer his brother. She wanted to answer it.

"It was that man you don't think's very bad. You know, the one you ain't never been scared of. Well I still think he's a bad man. It might just be me, but I still feel that way." If looks could kill, she would have dropped dead on the spot from the evil eyed look she got from her sometimes sex partner, Ace Brinlee.

John Wood had been lost in the dark woods for a half hour. While he was running away from Ace and Buford he really didn't care what direction he was headed. He was just scared and glad to get away. When he stopped he found himself in an area of the woods where he saw no familiar landmarks. There was nothing he recognized or that gave him his bearings at all.

John's eyes lit up and he smiled a smile of relief as he stepped out of the heavy woods into a clearing. He saw his first familiar sight and he knew he would be at the lodge soon if he followed the railroad track he had found. He looked up and saw the always dependable North star and began walking along the track in the direction of Roads End. John knew it had to be after midnight and he was now thirteen years old. He had faced Ace and Buford Brinlee and he was still alive. He did not run in fear as he lay on the ground and the huge freight train passed three feet away from him, making his body tremble and shaking the ground beneath him. He had enjoyed watching two grown women dance topless as the GTO car lights reflected off their bouncing breasts. "Satisfaction" by the Rolling Stones, would be his favorite song forever. The visions of the dancing beauties would last a lifetime and would be ignited every time he heard that song. And now he had been lost and he would find his own way home by the tracks and that beautiful star. It was a great night for a thirteen year old hunter from Roads End.

John's heart pounded in his chest when he looked up and saw

a set of headlights coming in his direction. His first thoughts were of the Brinlee brothers, but as the vehicle came closer he realized the Meatpacker's truck was coming to rescue him. The big truck lights lit up the ground and tracks around him as the truck stopped a few feet away. John knew he had everything under control and really didn't need to be rescued, but it would save him that long walk back to the lodge. Leon Barrett's voice sounded great as John stepped toward the truck. "You all right, boy?"

The purple Pontiac GTO was on the move. For the first time that night the two women were fully dressed. Buford Brinlee was in the back seat, with Lucy, as usual. There was no sexual activity at all. Lucy was sitting up and Buford was lying down with his head in her lap. He had his eyes closed and she rubbed his forehead with a gentle hand. Ace Brinlee was sitting in the passenger's seat up front. He had pushed the seat back to the reclined position. He had his eyes closed and he still had dirt caked on his face. There was no doubt both the Brinlee brothers were in pain. Molly was at the wheel of the GTO and it was her responsibility to get the evil siblings out of the woods and to the safety of their single wide trailer at the Whispering Pines Trailer Park in Woodbine, Georgia. Molly looked over at her pitiful boyfriend and shook her head. She cracked a little smile. "You all right, darlin'?" Ace didn't answer or open his eyes. She wouldn't ask again. The purple GTO moved toward Woodbine with two wild women and two beaten brothers.

The main room of the lodge was still buzzing about the huge poker hand Luther Reynolds had won with the once in a lifetime straight flush. The other players were licking their financial wounds and consoling each other about how close they had been to winning the hand themselves. Bill Wood thought perhaps a little cool fresh Georgia air would ease the pain he was feeling, so he walked to the front door and pushed it open, stepping out onto the concrete slab. He looked toward the dog pens in search of his son,

John and the other boys. Bill stepped off the concrete slab and walked to the edge of the building hoping to see John and the others sitting by the camp fire or in the back of one of the trucks. He wasn't really worried about John and the boys, because he knew they were somewhere close by, but he did want to say happy birthday to his now teenaged son. He turned toward the sound of a truck engine and saw a set of headlights coming through the main gate. As the truck rolled closer he could see Meatpacker and Leon sitting in the front seats and when the truck rolled to a stop he saw John and the other two boys sitting in the truck bed. As usual, the sight of John made his heart race and gave him great pleasure. The truck stopped a few feet away from the proud father.

"Kind'a cold to be ridin' back there, ain't it boys. Leon wouldn't let y'all jam in up front with him." Leon opened the passenger's side door and stepped out.

"No, sir, none of these boys sittin' in my lap, cold or not." Bill Wood walked around to the back of the truck where the three boys were climbing down.

"Happy Birthday, John!" John jumped to the ground and smiled at his father.

"Thanks, Daddy." Bill hugged John as the others watched. Bill had a father's question.

"Where y'all been, John? What y'all been up to with Meatpacker and Butch?" Meatpacker had gotten out of his truck and was walking past Bill. They were all surprised when Meatpacker answered Bill's question.

"Just took a loop in the woods, Bill. You know how a loop feels the night before the hunt. Just a little loop in the woods, that's all." Bill shook his head because he did understand how that felt. Leon smiled and the three boys realized they would only share the secrets of that night with the ones who were actually there. It was their adventure and even though the young men knew the adults would probably never discuss it again it would periodically pop into their heads with the slightest reminder. The song "Satisfaction" would be one of those reminders, every now and then. They all walked toward the warmth and safety of the Roads End hunting lodge. John looked at Jimbo and Little Mac as they moved to the concrete slab. They both looked at him too. John knew they wanted to know how he was able to escape from the evil clutches of the Brinlees. He knew they would all have to talk about it later. Raymond Lloyd stepped up next to Leon Barrett.

"Where'd ya leave your truck, Butch?"

"I think it's in Half Moon ditch. It was gettin' dark and I was in a hurry to get Mott off my hands. I'm sure it's in the front side of Half Moon." Meatpacker smiled.

"Let's go get it." Leon smiled too. Raymond Lloyd was a good friend. They left the others to their cards, drinking and stories.

The three young adventurers walked into the main building behind the adults. John Wood was the last to enter the room. His eyes popped open when he heard a thunder of male voices holler out, "Happy Birthday, John!" John stopped in his tracks as his father gave him a big hug and moved him to the big round wooden table. So far that night the table had served as a poker table with money piled high, a funeral ritual with cremated remains and now it was a table which would soon have John's birthday cake sitting in the middle where the Tupperware bowl had been. John was standing next to the table with a big smile on his face when the cook, Don Crawford, placed a two layer round spice cake with white icing in the middle of the table. It was plain with no decorations and the top layer of cake was leaning to one side making the cake look lopsided. It looked like the top layer would slide off at any moment. Don had a big smile and pleased look on his face when he placed the cake on the table. The spectators looked at the cake then at each other and then back at the cake. Luther Reynolds could not keep his thoughts to himself.

"What the hell happened to the cake?" Don's eyes lit up.

"Why? What's wrong?" Luther glared at Don.

"What's wrong? You mean you can't see the cake looks like it's gonna slide off the table at any second, now?" Don gave the cake a hard look. Luther couldn't help himself.

"You cock-eyed son-of-a-bitch. You think it's fine, don't ya?" Don looked at the other men as they all exploded with laughter at Luther's observation. Don looked at Luther.

"Maybe I need to look at it from another angle." The room exploded again. Luther shook his head.

"There ain't no better angle to look at it, Don. The angle's in the damn cake " Don looked at John.

"Sorry, John. I guess all this hollerin' and stompin' 'round here made it fall. I guess I was so excited 'bout gettin' it ready that I didn't take a good look at it." The room was silent. John smiled and put his arm around Don.

"It's the best birthday cake I've ever had. Thank you for thinking about me." Bill Wood was as proud of his thirteen year old son as he had ever been in his life. The moment of bonding was interrupted when Big John Blanyer stuck his huge Bowie hunting knife in the middle of the wooden table and added his thoughts to the birthday celebration.

"Let's quit bein' all mushy and cut that crooked son-of-a-bitch right now." Luther Reynolds had to give it to Don Crawford one more time.

"Which crooked son-of-a-bitch do you mean; the cake or the cook?" Don's eyes popped open and the room exploded with cheers and laughter. Don couldn't help but laugh at Luther's funny comment. Bill Wood laughed as loud as anyone and motioned for John to take the big knife and cut the wonderful, but lopsided, birthday cake. As John cut the cake his father placed a new shotgun on the table. John's eyes looked like they had sparklers in them. His entire face lit up. It was the most beautiful shotgun he had ever seen and a wonderful birthday gift on the eve of the hunting season. John didn't reach for the gift until his father nodded and John knew it was really his. This would be a night John Wood would never forget. It was great to be thirteen.

The purple Pontiac GTO, with the purple rubber goat hanging from the inside mirror, stopped at the gas pump at the Darien Truck Stop. Molly was still at the wheel and Ace Brinlee was still sitting in the passenger's bucket seat next to her. Ace turned to Buford, in the back seat.

"I'm gonna get this dirt off my face. Tell that retard, Clarence, to put five dollars worth in." Ace got out of the car. Molly had a thought.

"I'll pump it. I like pumpin' gas." Ace shook his head.

"How come that doesn't surprise me?" He looked back at Molly. "Stay in the car. Don't pump no gas." Molly stuck her bottom lip out like a child after Ace's instructions. Ace moved away from the car and went around the side of the main building of the truck stop. A tall young man in his twenties walked out of the building and stepped to the driver's side of the car, where the sexy Molly had her arm propped up in the window. Molly spoke first. "Hey Clarence, how you tonight?" The young man kept his head down and it was obvious he was not the best at talking to the ladies, especially a lady like Molly. From the back seat, Lucy added to his embarrassing moment.

"Heeeeey Clarence!" Clarence's head stayed down and Molly could see him tremble at the thought of talking to the women in the GTO.

"Damn, Lucy, he really likes you. He can't hold still after you said, 'hey'." Buford had heard enough. He sat up toward the front seat.

"Put five dollars regular in boy and quit talkin' to them women. You 'spose to be on the job." Molly looked at Buford.

"Quit talkin'? Buford, he ain't said a word to us. We was messin' with him. He ain't even looked at us."

"He's probably queer." Buford sat back in the seat. Clarence went to do his job and started pumping the gas into the purple "evil brother mobile". Molly had to keep talking.

"I don't think he's queer at all. He just ain't like other folks. Some people are shy and can't talk to other folks. It don't make 'em queer. He's probably a nice boy. He's always been nice when I've seen him." Buford didn't respond to Molly. He lay his head back on the back seat and closed his eyes. Molly watched Clarence in the rear view mirror as he took the gas nozzle out of the tank hole and placed it back on the pump. He walked back around to the driver's side window where Molly was waiting. Clarence stood there with his head down. Molly wanted to ease his nervousness.

"Ace will be back to pay you in a minute." Clarence kept his head down and spoke for the first time.

"Yes ma'am. Thank you." Molly smiled a beautiful white, straight toothed smile.

"You're welcome, Clarence." Clarence lifted his head and for the first time looked into Molly's eyes. Molly liked the bright gleam she saw in the young man's eyes. He shocked the three in the car when four slow words came out of Clarence's mouth.

"You sure are purdie." Molly smiled, but it was short lived when Ace grabbed Clarence from behind and threw him to the ground. Molly screamed as Clarence hit the ground. Ace went down and grabbed Clarence by his coat, lifting the young man off the ground and pulling him face-to-face.

"Who the hell do you think you are, talkin' to my woman like that? You must be the craziest retarded bastard on the earth." Ace pushed Clarence down again, as Molly jumped out of the car. Buford and Lucy followed Molly. Molly reached Ace as he reached for Clarence again. She grabbed Ace's arm and he turned back to her.

"This is crazy, Ace. Please don't do this." Ace's eyes glared with pure evil as if he were the devil himself. He put the palm of his hand in Molly's face and with a hard shove he pushed her to the ground next to the car. Molly's mini-skirt went up exposing the fact she wore no underwear. She hurried to pull her legs together and jumped up off the ground. Ace had turned back to the weaker and frightened Clarence as Buford came to his side.

"Ace, this boy ain't right. I'm scared you gonna kill 'im and we don't need that, do we. You been mad all night and it ain't got nothin' to do with this fool sayin' somethin' to Molly. It ain't his fault. The girl's were playin' him and he just fell into the play. He's a queer, can't you see that?" Buford took Ace by the arm and pulled him away from where he stood over Clarence. Molly stood at the front of the car. Ace turned to her.

"Get your ass back in the car. I'm drivin'." Molly's face showed her own evil glare for the first time that night.

"Ace, I can't let you do me like this anymore. You got some real problems and it's all because of that damn huntin' camp out there. You can't do anything to that big man out there, so you're beatin' up on people like Clarence and me. You ain't gonna hurt me no more. I ain't gettin' in the car. You go on, 'cause I ain't goin'." Ace's face continued to show his hatred, but he didn't respond at first. Molly wasn't through.

"Lucy, I'm sorry, but I hope you understand. I can't get back into that car." She looked at Buford. "Buford, you're right. He might just kill somebody and it could very well be me. Sorry to break up the evenin', but I'm scared standin' right here. I'm gonna be scared and lookin' over my shoulder for a long time 'cause I know Ace won't forget this. That's the way he lives. He only remembers the bad stuff, and he lives his life to get people back for what he thinks they have done to him. What an awful way to live. I been thinkin' what that big man said when he called us whores. I stuck my tits out the window and told him I wasn't no whore. But, it was pretty clear that's just what I am. I don't want to be part of it no more." Molly turned to walk toward the main building of the truck stop. Ace stepped toward her, but Buford held his arm. Ace looked up at his younger, but bigger brother. The evil glare was still there.

"I'm gonna kick her ass and then that retard's and then yours if I have to." Buford released his hold on his older, but smaller brother. Ace turned to where he had thrown Clarence. He was gone.

Ace turned to see Molly walk through the door of the truck stop. He walked quickly towards the door. Lucy and Buford stood next to the car. Lucy was worried about her friend Molly. As she watched, the more than despicable Ace Brinlee walked through the door and into the truck stop.

"Buford, do something, please. Don't let him hurt her." Buford took a deep breath.

"He ain't gonna hurt her in front of all those people in there. And if she don't get in the car, she'll be all right. He's just full of liquor and hate for Leon Barrett. I'll get him out of there." Buford left Lucy at the car and walked toward the front door.

Buford was about ten feet from the entrance of the building when his brother Ace came crashing through the wooden door, landing on the ground with pieces of the door all around him. Buford was shocked for the moment as Ace crawled up to his hands and knees. Ace Brinlee was dazed from the collision with the wooden door and the hard ground. Lucy's mouth dropped open and she couldn't believe her eyes. Buford stepped over to his injured brother as a group of men stomped through the broken door facing. Buford turned to defend himself and his fallen brother. The first three men Buford saw were the three young men who had left Roads End earlier that night in search of Georgia's dancing women. They didn't make it to Brunswick and it was a good thing for Molly they hadn't. Buford Brinlee found himself facing Clayton McKendree, Scott Milligan and Bruce Couey plus six other men who walked out of the building. Buford recognized the three members of Roads End. Scott Milligan was the spokesman.

"You need to get him out of here Buford. The young lady ain't goin' with y'all. We know how bad you boys think you are, but take a look around. You ain't that bad." Buford looked at the number of men standing in front of him and his brother. He knew they would have no chance if they tried to take Molly with them. He reached down and pulled Ace to his feet. Ace was still crazy with booze and hate.

"We can take 'em, Buford. They're a bunch of farmers." Buford moved his unrealistic older, but smaller, brother toward the car. Ace was too hurt and weak to resist Buford's controlling strength. They were near the GTO. Lucy opened the back door so Buford could put Ace into the car. Ace tried to turn back to the crowd of men.

"This ain't over, Roads End. Tell Barrett, I'm comin'." Lucy shook her head at Ace's obsession with Leon Barrett and the hunting camp. She looked toward the building and saw Molly standing at the window. Molly waved and Lucy waved back. They were good friends. The crowd of men turned back to the building as Buford dragged Ace into the back seat. Ace moaned in pain as Buford closed the back door. Lucy got into the car on the front passenger's side and Buford walked to the driver's side. Buford got into the car and it was the first time of the night that the two back seat lovers were up front. Buford looked back at Ace to see if he was alright before he started the GTO. When he turned back to start the car, Clarence was standing a few feet from the driver's side window. He stood there and stared at Buford Brinlee. Lucy looked past Buford and saw Clarence standing there. She smiled.

"Clarence, you O.K.?" Clarence licked his dry lips.

"I wanted him to know I ain't no queer."

Lopsided or not, John Wood's white icing spice cake was gone. The big Bowie knife lay on the table next to the plate of cake crumbs. White icing covered the wide steel blade. John was sitting near the large red brick fireplace. Little Mac and Jimbo sat with him. They were all admiring John's new shotgun and one of the supreme symbols of attaining Roads End manhood. Bill Wood watched his son, John, from across the large opened room. Bill did that quite often. The hunters who remained for the next morning's hunt and the opening day were getting settled in their barrack type rooms and preparing their beds.

The front door opened and another hunter walked into the building. It was Bill Wood's guest, Hugh Powell, from Jacksonville. Hugh had driven Bill's red Ford Bronco from Jacksonville. Bill met Hugh at the door with a big smile and a manly handshake for his friend from home.

"Well, I didn't think you were gonna come. Come on in. Welcome, welcome to Roads End." After Hugh Powell returned Bill's greeting and handshake, the newcomer followed Bill into the main room. Bill began introducing him to the regular members. He would be added to the long list of distinguished, and not so distinguished hunting guests who had graced the concrete slab and walls of the Roads End. Bill Wood would hunt with his son and friend in the morning and enjoy every minute of introducing Hugh to Bill's home away from home.

John watched his father as he moved his friend from member to member. John knew how proud and excited his father was to have Hugh Powell with him. Hugh was a member of the "He

Otter" hunting club on the South side of Jacksonville, Florida. Bill had been his guest at his club and now he was Bill's guest. Bill liked the name of the club. It had nothing to do with the fury little animal that plays in the creek waters. It meant, "He'otter be some place else."

The purple Pontiac GTO stopped next to Ace Brinlee's single wide trailer at the Whispering Pine Trailer Park. Buford got out of the driver's side and opened the back door to assist his older brother, Ace. He thought Ace needed help getting out of the back seat of the car. Buford reached into the car.

"Come on, Ace, we're at your place. Let's get you inside." Ace didn't reach out for Buford's hand.

"I don't need no damn help from you. You made me leave like I was a coward. We should'a stayed. I hate them farmers. Leave me be, dammit." Buford stepped away from the back door of the car as Lucy joined him.

"I need to get on home, Buford. You want me to just take your car or you gonna take me? It don't make no difference to me. If ya need to stay with Ace go ahead, but I'm gone." Buford nodded his head. Lucy wasn't finished. "Ya think I should go back and get Molly? I'm worried about her." Ace answered Lucy's question from the back seat.

"That bitch will get a ride, she's probably got her head between one of those farmer's legs right now." Lucy looked toward the back seat, but didn't respond to his nasty comment about her friend. She looked at Buford.

"Well, what do you want me to do?" Buford wanted to be with Lucy much more than he wanted to be with his brother.

"Let me get him inside and I'll take you home." Lucy nodded her head and she felt good about Buford's decision. Buford moved back to the back door of the car.

"Come on, Ace. Go on inside. I'm gonna take Lucy home." Ace

moved to the edge of the back seat and put his feet on the ground.

"Just give me the keys. I can go into the house without you. Take her on home. I can take care of myself." Buford knew there was no sense in trying to be reasonable with the unreasonable Ace Brinlee. He handed the keys to the GTO and the trailer to Ace and walked to his black Ford Cyclone GT, where Lucy was waiting by the passenger's side door. Buford unlocked the door for Lucy and opened the door for her. He closed the door and walked around to the driver's side. He got into the front seat and started the Cyclone motor. The car rocked from side-to-side as Buford warmed up the monster engine. Lucy smiled. She liked the feeling of the seat vibrating under her and how it made the cheeks of her butt shake and tingle. Buford looked out of the front windshield as Ace made his way slowly to the metal steps of his trailer. Lucy continued to watch as Ace was able to finally move up the three steps, open the narrow door and stumble into the trailer. The Ford Cyclone was on the move.

The first big poker game of the new season had ended rather early in comparison to previous years, with the old pissbird, himself, cleaning the clocks and the wallets of the other six high rollers who had experienced the misfortune of having a seat at Luther Reynolds' table of doom. No other group had stepped up to fill the chairs for a second game as Friday night passed and the Saturday morning hours enveloped Roads End. It was unusual for the games not to continue into the early morning hours, but the humdinger status of the first game had drained the life from the normal participants. The losers had not yet recovered mentally and would not recover financially any time soon. Raymond Lloyd pushed the gas peddle of his truck down with his big foot. With slightly spinning tires and raw power, his vehicle pulled Leon's truck out of the water filled ditch. They would both be back at the lodge in a few minutes.

The big black and white clock on the kitchen wall let everyone know it was two A.M. and hunting time for the new season was just a few hours away. With only twenty-two adult hunters and three young teenage boys, there was plenty of space in the ten bedrooms. Each room had two sets of bunkbeds so four people could sleep in each room. The three young men were all assigned to one room and they were preparing their bunks when Bill Wood stepped to the door of the room. John turned to the door when he heard his father's voice.

"John, you boys gonna be alright in here?" They all nodded and answered "yes, sir" at the same time. "At least you boys won't have to sleep with some of these old timers who snore like freight trains, but maybe y'all snore too." Bill looked at the bottom bunk where John was sitting. "You need to get on the top bunk, son. You see those concrete cinder blocks under that bed?" John and the others boys looked at the concrete blocks they had not noticed before. "Those blocks have been stacked there to hold Chuck "Haystacks" Drew, all four hundred pounds of him, if he makes it here from Mayport for the morning hunt." Six young eyes were wide open as Bill continued. "He'll probably be here in the morning or later on tonight. So, no sense in you having to move to the top bunk in the middle of the night. Get on up top and get used to sleeping up there. Old Haystacks will be y'all's fourth."

The boys were silent as they looked at the blocks and at each other. The six concrete blocks were distributed under the bed so the wooden base and cross slats were supported by the blocks. The boys knew what the blocks were for. They had no idea they had chosen the room where the four hundred pounder would lay his huge head on a pillow some time during the weekend. All three boys knew the tales about sleeping in the same room with the "Fatman". Bill pointed to a large Mason jar sitting on a two-by-four wall board and added to the boys' discomfort.

"See there? That's his piss jar up there on the wall." The three boys looked at the yellow stained glass container. "You boys have to remember, when you are that big you can't be getting up and down out of bed during the night. Once he's in bed he's usually there to stay until morning. So when he has to go, he pees in that jar and empties it each morning. So any time during the night you might think it's raining, it's probably just ol' Haystacks takin' a big leak, because a man like him don't do nothin' little." Bill Wood fought back a smile as he looked into the faces of the three shocked boys. He knew he had given them food for crazy thoughts and most likely a sleepless night anticipating the arrival of their fourth roommate. The three boys all had the same thoughts of the Fatman relieving himself while in the prone position in the bed nearby. John had to ask his father a question.

"You think he's comin' in, Daddy?" All six eyes wanted to know.

"He'll be here all right. He's not gonna miss an opening day. Not the Fatman." Bill's answer wasn't even close to what the three boys wanted to hear. Bill left them with a "good night" and a "happy birthday, John."

The movement, noise and excitement of the main room was calming as the true hunters knew they had to get some sleep before they were back up at the crack of dawn, if not earlier. The veterans knew even a little sleep was always better than none at all. Bill walked to his room where his guest was unloading his duffle bag. No one would sleep in Jim Mott's bunk during that hunting season, but come next year's opening day a new member would be sleeping and snoring in Jim's old bed. Jim would understand and wouldn't have it any other way.

Leon Barrett walked into his room where his uncle, James Reynolds, was already snoring and Chief Luther Reynolds was dead asleep with his winnings from the poker table piled all over his bed, covering him like a green presidential picture blanket.

Leon smiled at the old man's sense of humor, his trust of his fellow man, and his devil may care attitude. Leon knew no member of the lodge would touch the money, even in jest, but it was still a crazy sight to see all Luther's winnings displayed in such a manner. Luther Reynolds was living his life for the moment and it was obvious he had few worries. Raymond "Meatpacker" Lloyd joined Leon at the door of the room.

"Would you look at that crazy old bastard. He don't give a rat's ass 'bout anything, does he?" Leon smiled again and shook his head.

"Not that I've seen. But, he is funny, ain't he?"

The front door of the lodge opened and the three young "Molly rescuers" had returned from Darien. They were red faced and a little shaky as they walked, but they were all safe and ready for bed. Leon nodded to all three of them as they walked past him and Meatpacker. They turned to their room. Bruce Couey looked back at Leon in the doorway.

"Ace Brinlee said to tell you he's comin'." Leon looked at the messenger and shook his head.

"Well, he better get here quick, 'cause I'm goin' to bed."

The only light left on at the Roads End hunting lodge was the light in the kitchen so the night walkers would be able to see where they were going if they began to roam during the night. With that many men sleeping in one place, there would always be reasons to walk during the wee hours. The nights at Roads End were never really restful unless you had gotten used to the many noises of such a place. The barking dogs, train whistles, engines roaring, snoring, other bodily functions and the sounds of the creatures of the night kept many night walkers on the move at different hours throughout the night.

The camp had been settled for half an hour. John Wood stared at the ceiling above the top bunk. He was still wide awake. He didn't think the other boys were sleeping either, but they had stopped talking and actually seemed to be trying to fall asleep. The sound of one of the members coughing echoed down the empty hall of the large building. The wild excitement of the evening flashed in John's thirteen year old head.

John thought about his birthday cake and the topless women dancing in the woods. He thought about his new shotgun, the morning hunt, and the topless dancers in front of the car lights. He thought about being face-to-face with the devil, Ace Brinlee, and the topless dancing women in the woods. If he did fall asleep he knew what he wanted to dream about and it had nothing to do with deer hunting.

The black Ford Cyclone GT pulled away from the Darien Truck Stop. Buford Brinlee was at the wheel. Lucy was in the front bucket seat beside him and Molly was sitting in the back seat. Molly was glad to see Lucy and Buford.

"I really do appreciate y'all comin' back for me like this. I'm sorry Buford 'bout what happened." Buford nodded, but didn't say anything. He kept his hand on the wheel and eye on the road. Molly knew Buford would not be part of any talk against his brother, Ace, so she didn't talk about the earlier incident. Lucy was concerned.

"Are ya hurt, Molly?" Buford looked into the rearview mirror into the back seat and then back at the road.

"I'm just a little bruised and embarrassed about the whole thing. Ace really scares me and I just got scared. We all had too much to drink. My head ain't cleared yet." Lucy smiled.

"Mine either." Molly had to ask.

"Where is Ace, anyway?" Buford looked into the mirror again at Molly in the back seat. Lucy responded.

"He's back at the trailer sleepin' it off."

"Did he get hurt? He looked hurt to me." Buford had the answer.

"Just a little bruised and embarrassed." He smiled at Molly in the mirror. She smiled back at him and his comment gave her some relief from the strange feeling she had in her awkward situation. She wasn't sure how Buford would react to her. She knew how dedicated he was to his older brother. Molly took Buford's comment as his saying things are all right. She sat back in the seat and kept quiet. She knew Buford would take her and Lucy home.

John Wood's eyes popped open when light from a truck bounced off the wall next to his top bunk. When he sat up and crawled to the window he realized the other two boys were sound asleep. A huge red F350 Ford pickup truck with monster oversized tires rolled through the main gate and up to the edge of the concrete slab. The engine went silent and the light on the inside of the truck flashed brightly when the driver opened the door. John couldn't see who it was, but he had a feeling the slow moving, huge shadow of a figure stepping down from that truck was none other than the Fatman himself, Chuck "Haystacks" Drew, the shrimper from Mayport.

When the man turned, walked around the front of the truck, then stepped up onto the concrete slab, John knew his roommate and bottom bunk sleeping partner had arrived and was headed in his direction. John's throat went dry and he pushed his body back into the pillow he had left to look out the window. He wished he had fallen asleep, but it was definitely too late for that. He heard the front door open and close. John listened for heavy footsteps, but he heard none. He listened harder and still nothing. A hot liquid filled John's throat when he looked at the door which suddenly opened and spilled muted light into the room as a huge shadow loomed to cover the entire door facing. The Fatman was standing in the doorway. John had no idea how a man that size could have been so light on his feet as he made his way down the hall to the room. John didn't want to think the Fatman was actually trying to

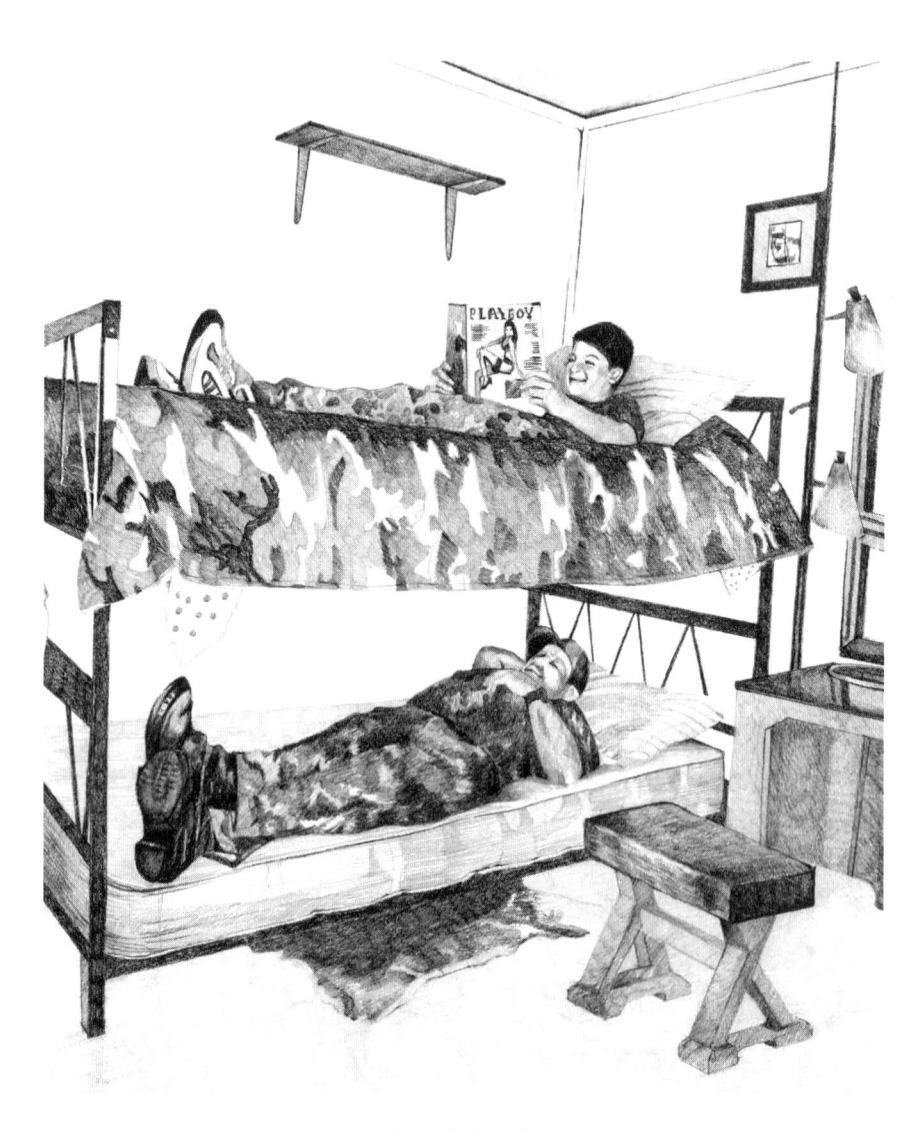

Bunk Beds

sneak up on him. It was too dark in the room for Haystacks to see who was in the other bunks. He really didn't care. The moonlight coming through the window gave him enough light to see that his bed was empty and waiting for him.

John pretended to be sleeping as the Fatman entered the room and sat down on the edge of the concrete block supported bed. John's top bunk swayed from side-to-side with a creaking noise when Haystacks put all his four hundred pounds down on the thin mattress on the blocks and bed frame. Jimbo and Little Mac suddenly awakened, but like John, they didn't move either. Haystacks moaned when he bent over to take his boots off. John knew the second Haystacks removed his boots. The odor of the Fatman's feet emanated from his socks and boots. All three boys buried their heads into their pillows as the suffocating odor permeated the small room. The bunkbed moved and rocked as the Fatman settled himself onto a prone position on his back. Haystacks didn't care who his roommates were. He was just happy to be off his feet. To be off his feet was one of his great pleasures. The only one who would sleep well in the room that night was the last one who arrived. The Fatman was snoring in a matter of minutes.

The black Ford Cyclone GT stopped in front of Molly's little A-Framed Jim Walter house. Molly's mother had given her a half acre of land and she had used the deed to the land to finance building the house. Lucy was her roommate for the time being. Molly opened the back door and got out on the driver's side of the car. She stepped to the window where Buford sat at the wheel.

"Thanks for coming back for me, Buford. It was a nice thing to do." Buford nodded and Molly walked to her front porch. Lucy leaned over to Buford and gave him a hard passionate kiss. He squeezed one of her breasts as she buried her face into his. Lucy pushed against him and rubbed him between his legs. Molly went into the house. She knew Lucy would be coming in later.

John Wood looked over at Little Mac on the top bunk across from him. There was enough light from outside for him to see Little Mac's wide open eyes. It was too dark below to see Jimbo, but John knew he had to be awake too. The noises coming from the bottom bunk under John, were outrageous. The stomach rumbles, nose snorting, and painful moans and groans were pounding John's head. He even thought about leaving the room and sleeping on the couch up front in the main room, or even finding another bed in another room. He even considered one of the trucks outside. John was just about to make his move and climb to the floor when a strange sound filled the hallway next to their room.

John didn't know who was making the strange noise, but the older members knew it was Lester Rowe having one of his early morning anxiety attacks. Lester was prone to such outbursts after he had indulged in the Wild Turkey and fallen asleep. It seemed Lester was plagued with nightmares and every now and then he would kick, yell, fight and agonize in his sleep before he would jump out of bed and run through the building as if he was being chased by the demons of the woods. His wild uncontrollable delirium would wake even the deepest sleeper in the camp, causing a number of the hunters to chase him down and wake him up before he hurt himself. John heard the others in the hall as they were able the calm the first night walker of the night. He couldn't see who was helping Lester back to his room. Lester Rowe was embarrassed, but he was headed back to bed.

The four loudest and most annoying snorers were Lonnie Sikes, Gus Guthrie, Edgar Masters and the world class, and could have been Olympic gold medalist, Dallas Thomas. Dallas would have been the captain of the United States Olympic snoring team, if the country needed him. He would have gone too. He was very patriotic.

Dallas was the true king. He was the Elvis of nasal congestion.

To say he had a deviated septum was a gross understatement. He most likely had no septum to deviate at all. It was rather scary for the other members to hear Dallas, during the night, struggling for air as he slept. His snoring was a mixture of short choppy snorts, wheezing and actual choking. It compared to a death rattle from a horror movie or some of the noises heard at John King's haunted house in Mayport, Florida. At times he was thought to be dead in his bed when a long, breathless silence would prevail after one of his indescribable barrages of horrifying noises.

John lay back on his pillow and looked at the ceiling. He was living his own nightmare, but he was awake during it. The nightmare would continue when John realized there was movement below him in the bottom bunk. He wasn't sure how he knew, but he knew the Fatman was sitting up in his bed and John knew Haystacks was reaching for the large Mason piss jar next to the bed. John felt it when Haystacks lay back and rolled over onto his side. John visualized the Mason jar being placed between those huge legs. The one thing John didn't realize was that as he visualized what was happening below him, Jimbo and Little Mac were actually watching it take place. The next thing that happened could never be explained. It was the sound of Chuck "Haystacks" Drew urinating into the Mason jar. The Fatman's loud sigh of pure relief added to the unforgettable moment for the three young hunters. They could hear the glass jar filling and it seemed like the sound would never stop. The boys all wondered just how much the stained jar would hold. It sounded like it was near capacity and possibly moving into the overflow mode, when it stopped. Then there were a few shots, splashes and several drips. The awful experience was over. Haystacks sat up and placed the open jar back onto the two-by-four cross brace next to his bunk. The boys found themselves in young hunter's hell as Haystacks rolled over, broke wind like an elephant, which seemed to rattle the walls of the small room, then fell back to a dead sleep.

A flash of lightning lit up the small bedroom. John wasn't sure if he had dropped off to sleep for a minute, but he was awake again. The crack of thunder followed the flash. John thought he must have fallen asleep because he did not know it had been raining until that moment. There were voices in the hallway and farther away near the kitchen area. There was movement on the other side of the room. John looked in that direction and saw Little Mac climb down off his top bunk and leave the room.

Little Mac walked into the latrine and positioned himself in front of one of the three urinals. He had no idea there was someone sitting on one of the exposed toilets behind him. Little Mac began to relieve himself when a deep voice from behind sent a sharp pain through his young heart.

"That hard rain's gonna make this first hunt a muddy one, ain't it?" Little Mac's heart raced and he was frozen with fear. He held himself with a trembling hand as he finished his personal morning business. Little Mac did not want to be in that room with someone sitting on the toilet, having a conversation in the dark of the early morning. He didn't even know who it was yet. His agony continued.

"Who's boy are you?" Little Mac knew he would have to talk to the mystery voice behind him. He was finished, but pretended not to be. He took a deep breath that he realized was a mistake, as soon as he did it. He continued facing the wall over the urinal.

"I'm Tom McGehee's son, Mac. They call me Little Mac."
"I know your daddy good. We go way back. You boys sure grow up fast." Little Mac knew he would have to turn and face the man behind him. He turned to see an incredible sight.

It was the Fatman, himself. Little Mac had never seen anything like it in his young life, and he knew instantly he never wanted to see it again. Haystacks was completely naked except for a huge pair of powder blue boxer shorts that lay on the floor covering his big feet. Both sides of his butt cheeks actually hung over the sides of the toilet bowl. The bowl was completely covered and no white porcelain was visible. It looked as if the Fatman was hovering in the air with nothing supporting his massive body. Little Mac was sure Haystacks' head weighed a hundred pounds alone. He was mesmerized by the sight before him.

"Damn boy, you all right?" Little Mac nodded his head and walked out of the latrine. He would never forget the vision of the Fatman sitting on the invisible porcelain throne.

John and Jimbo were standing at the door of their bedroom as Little Mac returned from his adventure with the Fatman. He had words of wisdom and good advice for his two young friends. "Don't go to the bathroom right now. Trust me."

Don Crawford dropped bacon strips into the big, black iron frying pan and it began to sizzle. The aroma instantly filled the air in the kitchen, hall and the ten bedrooms. Nothing travels faster than the smell of bacon cooking and coffee brewing in the morning. The sun was still hidden, but was on its way.

The members and guests of Roads End began to leave their beds and fill the hall and main room of the building. The boys joined the movement in the hall. As they approached the door of the latrine, Haystacks walked out of the door and into the hall in front of them. They all stopped in their tracks when they saw the huge man standing there in the biggest pair of blue boxer shorts they had ever seen and would probably ever see again. Haystacks gave the boys a big smile and morning greeting.

"I hope I didn't wake you boys comin' in so late last night. Y'all sure was deep and quiet sleepers. I really like havin' you boys as roommates. I'll be able to get some rest for a change around here.

Hell, it's awful tryin' to get any sleep with some of the ol' timers around here, if ya know what I mean. Let me get some clothes on. That damn bacon's callin' my name." The three young hunters moved against the wall of the hallway to let the Fatman go by. They were speechless as he went past them and to the bedroom. Jimbo and John hurried to the urinals. Little Mac went to the kitchen.

Don Crawford was in culinary heaven as he emptied pots and pans full of breakfast food into plates and bowls, creating a early morning bonanza for the small army of hunters. The true cooks of the world live for such moments. The aroma that was taking over the entire building announced the opening of the new hunting season in the Georgia woods at Roads End. Some of the men sat down, talked, laughed and ate their breakfast at the table. Some took a plateful outside and sat on the concrete slab. Some just wrapped a piece of toast around a strip of bacon and went out to get ready for the day in the woods.

The heavy rain had left its mark on the low areas of the front yard and near the dog pens, where most of the dirt was visible. A few mud puddles dotted the walk to the dog pens, but no one seemed to notice or care. The dogs, sensing the run and hunt, began to bark, howl and make their desires and presence known to any deer in the immediate area. Jimmy Carter was the first to stand with his dogs. He loved his dogs and always had the most to run. Everyone expected Jimmy and his dogs to set the pace and lead the way.

Leon Barrett stepped off the concrete slab and walked toward the dog pens. He passed Bill Wood standing next to a red Bronco with his guest, Hugh Powell. The world famous or at least the Roads End famous, Bullet, the beagle hound, stood on the hood of the vehicle. Bill Wood loved that dog. You could see it in his eyes. Leon stopped to pet and admire Bill's favorite runner.

"Ol' Bullet's lookin' fit, Bill. He always has that ready look, don't he?" Bill Wood was beaming. You would have thought Leon was talking about Bill's son, John. Bill responded.

"He's always ready, that's a fact. I didn't like that toad buster coming in last night. I worry about the dogs after a down pour. I think about the Northeaster we had a few years ago and how it drove the rattle snakes out of their dens and holes. I'll be worried all day." Leon nodded.

"Between the snakes and the trains runnin' through, we'll all be worried." Bill was curious.

"I didn't see Bud Bo in the pens. He all right?" It was Leon's turn to beam.

"I hope Ed and Ramsey bring him in shortly. Donny Carter's bringin' the boys with him. They should have been here by now." Bud Bo was Leon's pit bull and favorite hunting companion. Bill loved talking about his favorite, Bullet.

"My wife, Thelma, told me she thought I loved Bullet more than I loved her, but I told her she was absolutely wrong and that I loved her just as much as I love that dog." Leon had to laugh out loud at Bill's little joke. Bill wasn't finished with his praise for the ultimate beagle hound. "Ol' Bullet's only got three minor faults as dogs go, that I can see. He hasn't learned to distinguish the does from the bucks. He won't stay with a deer that's been killed in front of him. And he hasn't quite mastered good English. He frequently uses bad grammar and slang, especially when someone catches him cheating at poker." Leon laughed again. Bill Wood was in rare form. He did love that first morning as they all prepared for the hunt. Just being there at Roads End lifted his spirits and he was always willing to share his "feel good" moments and thoughts with anyone near by. Jimmy Carter had been listening to the talk about the dogs and, like Bill and Leon, it was one of Jimmy's favorite subjects too. He joined them at the red Bronco.

"Nothin's more heartbreakin' then hearin' that damn train

whistle blowin' as that engineer tries to get a dog off the tracks. It makes me sick to my stomach every time I hear it. Hell, I lost three dogs last year in two days." Bill and Leon nodded at the same time as Jimmy's reminder made them remember that sad time. Bill consoled Jimmy.

"I don't know how you handled it, Jimmy. It was a sad day for us all." Jimmy had more thoughts of that awful day.

"As smart as those dogs are, you'd think they would jump off the track when that whistle sounds, wouldn't ya. But, for some reason they always stay inside the rails and run dead ahead, tryin' to outrun the damn train. I don't understand it. Never will."

Dog runners have to be ready and geared for tragedies if they continue to take their dogs to the woods. It's part of the hunt, but it's never easy on the true dog lover. Bill Wood shared his thoughts with his fellow hunters and dog lovers.

"Don't tell the others I said this, but one of my favorite parts of the hunt is finding our lost dogs." Leon and Jimmy smiled at Bill's true confession moment. They knew what Bill meant by such a statement. Bill was on a roll.

"I like celebrating with a shot of scotch after we find and box one. It always seems the dogs we want to find are the hardest, and the least we want to find are the easiest to find. Hell, Mott's not worth a damn, Fartblossom was so easy to find we knew we could use her for a reason to take another drink." Leon and Jimmy smiled again as Bill continued his walk down dog running memory lane.

"Sometimes we've had to travel darn near Brunswick to find Ol' Bob a time or two. That damn dog would stay out two, three days at a time. I never will forget the day that monster rattle snake put down Howard Smith's big registered blue tick hound. Those fangs caught him right in his throat. That dog's head swelled up to three times its normal size before he died. It took an entire quart of

Ancient Age bourbon to console Howard and put him to sleep that night." The sound of a horn blowing took Bill's attention, as well as the other's. They all turned to the front gate to see an old rusty Ford panel truck. Leon smiled because he knew Donny Carter was bringing his two sons, Ed and Ramsey, into the camp to hunt with their father. Leon's grin got even bigger when he saw Bud Bo's box in the back of the truck.

"All right. My three boys are here." Bill and Jimmy smiled. They knew Leon had added Bud Bo to his family. Leon moved away from the red Bronco to meet the panel truck.

Bill Wood didn't see him when he pulled into camp, but he was always glad to see his friend, Charlie Jefferson. Charlie had brought his two sons, Wayne-O and Jeramie. Wayne-O was eight and Jeramie was six. They would be the youngest boys to be in camp for that particular opening weekend. They were quiet, good boys with polite manners and respect for the other members. Charlie had done a good job raising his two young sons. They would be great future members at Roads End. Bill knew they wouldn't be any trouble. They would stay close to their father. He waved to his friend and the boys.

Bill Wood and Hugh Powell moved to the concrete slab to pick up their equipment and started loading the red Bronco. John Wood came out of the building to help his father with the equipment. Another truck drove through the main gate. Bill looked at the truck and he knew everyone's favorite veterinarian, S. T. "Doc" Johnson, was bringing his most welcomed skills and expertise with him. Bill also noticed another member of Roads End was sitting in the passenger's seat of Doc's truck. The dark and handsome, Tom Cravey, had arrived. Tom stepped out of the passenger's side and Doc stepped out of the driver's side of the car. Bill Wood greeted them first.

"Damn, Doc, you don't care who you let ride in your car, do ya.

I always thought you had better judgement than that." Tom Cravey's eyes lit up as Doc responded.

"I thought he was injured by the road, but when I stopped I could see he was a road kill. It's my duty as a physician to bring him in. In other words, it was a mercy ride." The men within hearing distance all laughed at Doc's early morning sense of humor. Tom didn't smile or laugh, he just shook his head. Bill walked to Tom and put his arm around his curly headed friend.

"Don's got some of his "cat head" biscuits waitin' just for you, you handsome devil." Tom was too cool for all their foolishness. He just shook his head and went looking for those big flaky cat heads.

All the members had a good feeling when Doc was in the camp. His professional advice and care had saved many beloved hunting dogs, including one of Bill Wood's favorites, Lady, when she was ripped up the middle by a big wild boar two years before. Doc Johnson had a knack for catching shy dogs and he would rather ride the roads finding lost dogs than carry a gun. He was a slow talking man whom they all liked and respected.

All the hunters, who had stayed the night, had eaten their fill of Don Crawford's great breakfast. Tom Cravey had eaten the last two cat head biscuits covered with honey. Don and the three young teenagers were cleaning the kitchen area as the other hunters were gathering their hunting gear for the all day hunt. Everybody did their share at Roads End.

Leon Barrett stood next to Donny Carter's truck with his sons, Ed and Ramsey. Ed was sixteen and Ramsey was thirteen. John Wood, Jimbo Carter and Little Mac McGehee would be glad to see the young Barrett brothers and add them to the group of teenage hunters for the opening day. Leon hugged his two sons and moved to the back of the truck to take his pit bull, Bud Bo, out of his box and allow the dog to stretch its legs and run free in the main yard.

Bud Bo ran between the trucks and other vehicles, around the many hunters, over to the dog pens, where he got all the dogs barking again, and then back to his master. Leon knew Bud Bo would stay close to him and the boys. Bill Wood had to comment.

"I think Bud Bo's as ready as any of us, don't you?" Leon smiled as the excited dog ran past them again.

"I think you're right." Leon turned to Ed and Ramsey. "I didn't think y'all were gonna make it in time. We're almost ready to head out. Y'all got everything ya need?" Ed and Ramsey said, "yes sir" at the same time. Leon smiled again and looked at Donny Carter. "Thanks for bringin' 'em in, Donny."

"No problem, Butch. We had fun talkin' 'bout their daddy all the way here." Leon turned to Ed and Ramsey and put them both in a head lock; one under each big arm.

"Talkin' 'bout your ol' man, huh?" Two muffled voices said, "No, sir," at the same time. As Leon released his two sons, Little Mac and Jimbo walked up to the truck. Little Mac greeted the two new additions to the teenage hunters.

"You two should have been here last night. Y'all missed it." Somebody always has to tell you about something you missed. Ed and Ramsey moved away with Jimbo and Little Mac. They wanted to be filled in on what they had missed. Ed Barrett had the first question for the other two.

"Any Playboys in there?" It was a good question. Jimbo and Little Mac had to think for a second. Jimbo responded.

"Ya know, I haven't seen any at all. I hadn't thought about it, but they must have put them all away for some reason. I can't believe I didn't see any." Little Mac knew why they hadn't looked for the treasured "educational" magazines.

"We didn't need to see no pictures last night. We saw the real thing up close and in person." Ed and Ramsey looked at Jimbo, hoping he would know what Little Mac was referring to. Jimbo didn't let them down as he supported and enhanced Little Mac's vague explanation of what happened the night before.

"He's right. I guess I didn't think about the Playboys 'cause we saw real live titties in the woods last night. Then a real naked woman jumped up from behind a bush. And then the two women danced with no shirts on. Then the naked woman from the bush stood by the truck and talked to your daddy. Then your daddy hit Ace Brinlee in the back with an ax handle and knocked him into the water. Then your daddy jumped out of the truck and knocked the other Brinlee brother to the ground. That's when the naked lady talked to him. And the Brinlees captured John. You know John Wood. They captured all three of us first, but me and Little Mac got away and took your daddy and Meatpacker back to where they had John. That's when the lady jumped from behind the bush. We got captured while we were watchin' the women dance in the woods with no shirts on." Ed and Ramsey's eyes and mouths were wide open. It was impossible for them to take in all that Jimbo had handed them. The story about the naked and dancing women was wild enough, but the fact that Jimbo kept adding their father to the mix was just too much for them both. John Wood joined the foursome and they all walked toward the dog pens.

The full circle of the beautiful orange Georgia morning sun was visible in the eastern sky. The rain clouds were gone. It would be a cold, but clear day. The front yard of the camp had the look of an army immobilizing for war. There were big trucks, Jeeps and enough visible fire power to defend Roads End from all hostile invaders. The action and excitement of the night before was doubled on the actual day of the hunt. Bill Wood stood on the concrete slab and watched the wonderful movement and action he dearly loved. He was in Roads End heaven and he was bathing in every second of the moment.

Leon Barrett stood with Doc Johnson, Tom Cravey and Donny Carter, the three late additions to the hunt. Tom Cravey had the floor. "I'm sorry I didn't get here last night for the ceremony. I had good intentions. They just didn't work out." Donny Carter didn't say anything. Doc Johnson felt bad, like Tom, about not being there.

"I had emergencies all day. Seems like everything was life threatening." Leon really didn't know what to say, but he tried.

"It was your typical, Jim Mott blowout." They all smiled. Leon had no idea his image was reflecting on the round glass and cross bars of the scope of a high powered thirty-thirty automatic rifle with Ace Brinlee's eye pressed against the other end of the scope. Ace Brinlee pulled the trigger of the unloaded gun, clicked it three times and talked to himself.

"I got ya, Leon. Anytime I want ya, I got ya." He looked through the scope again and scanned the entire front yard, stopping on one hunter and then moving to another. He continued talking to himself and held the rifle between the forked limb of a tree.

"I got you. I got you." The lens of the scope found Bill Wood. Ace kept talking. "I don't know who I hate more, you or Barrett. I guess it's Barrett. But, I got you too, if I want ya. I should'a kicked that boy of yours little ass last night. I can't believe I let Buford talk me into letting him go. I won't do that next time." Ace pulled the gun from its resting spot in the tree and walked away from his sniper position. He walked a few yards through the woods to where the purple Pontiac GTO was parked and hidden on one of the old hunter's trails that divided the hunting blocks at Roads End.

The army of deer hunters was ready to take to the fields of battle. All vehicles were lined up one by one behind Leon Barrett's truck in the lead position. He was to be the "Huntmaster" for the opening weekend and he would not only lead the procession, but he would also assign the blocks for each individual group of hunters.

"Got Ya"

The green monster, open-sided Jeep with Luther Reynolds at the wheel pulled up next to Leon's lead truck. Leon looked into the passenger's side of the green monster and saw his Uncle James Reynolds sitting up tall in the seat. He looked across to the driver's side and saw Luther Reynolds.

"What's this? The Reynolds boys huntin' together today?" Uncle James gave a big smile.

"We know it ain't fair to you youngins, but we don't give a rat's ass 'bout y'all." Luther Reynolds had to add his two cents from the driver's side.

"That's right, boy. We gonna give all you pissbirds a lesson in becomin' one with the woods. A huntin' clinic, if you will. You must become the trees and be one with nature." Leon couldn't resist.

"You been watchin' too much of that Kung Fu on TV, Mister Luther. You'll be askin' us to snatch a pebble out of your hand, next. " Luther Reynolds smiled and blew smoke from his mouth without removing the big cigar.

"I don't know 'bout no pebble, but you can snatch a pissbird out my ass if you get a chance." The two old timers laughed out loud, trying to get Leon back for his earlier joke on them. Leon smiled, shook his head and looked into the back of the Jeep. He saw Dallas Thomas and Leonard Hooks sitting in the small, cramped back seat.

"Damn, you got all the old men with ya, today. Y'all got enough Geritol to pass around and last the whole day. The youngest one in that ugly green machine is at least a hundred, ain't he? " They all laughed at Leon's observation. They didn't want to, but they couldn't help it. They all knew when something was funny and were always looking for a good laugh at anyone's expense, even their own. Uncle James had to respond to his favorite nephew.

"And don't take that damn shortcut on that No-Go Road, like ya did last time you were the Huntmaster. Ya' damn near got us all killed on the clay road. And with that heavy rain last night, that clay on No-Go will be slicker than owl-shit and we'll spend the day pullin' all this rollin' stock out of the mud and the clay. You do understand why they call it No-Go, don't ya?" Ed and Ramsey both laughed out loud when their Uncle James said, "slicker than owl-shit." He did sound funny when he talked. Leon smiled at his uncle's funny reprimand. He did love his Uncle James. Leon started the engine of his truck and looked back at his Uncle James. "No-go on No-Go." Leon blew the horn on his truck as a signal to the others and drove though the main gate with Ed and Ramsey next to him in the cab. Ramsey noticed something strange and had a question for his father.

"Daddy, what's that grey dust doin' on the floor, over here? It looks funny." Leon had forgotten about the minor accident and major spill on the floor of his truck that had occurred the night before. He looked at Ramsey's "waiting for an answer" face.

"It's dried up dirt, I guess." Ed looked down on the floor.

"It don't look like dirt, daddy. It looks like ashes, like somethin' was burned down there." Leon looked out the front window.

"It's probably just sand."

Jimbo Carter was riding with his father. John Wood was riding with his father. Little Mac McGehee was riding with his father. And Ed and Ramsey Barrett were riding with their father and what was left of Jim Mott. It was the way it was supposed to be at Roads End.

The army of deer hunters had no idea how wild their first day in the woods was going to be. If they had known what was in store for them, perhaps they would have remained at the camp and played cards all day, but probably not. Even Lester Rowe had eaten a great breakfast and was ready to hunt. He would sweat out the river of Wild Turkey he had consumed the night before. He would smell like liquor all day, as the fumes actually passed through the pores of his body. Lester had suffered for years with excruciating and unrelenting headaches. Perhaps the painful headaches came from his heavy drinking or perhaps he drank because of the awful headaches. Either way, the hunters at Roads End were much safer in the woods when Lester Rowe was sleeping it off back at the lodge. To have Lester in your hunting party only added to one's possibility of being accidentally shot during one of the more confusing moments during the hunt.

Big John Blanyer looked back through the rear window of his truck and smiled at Lester Rowe sitting in the back bed of the truck. Big John knew Lester already had one of his bad headaches when Lester squinted his eyes in place of a smile.

"You alright back there, Lester?" Lester kept his head down.

"Except for my head feelin' like it's gonna explode, I'm just fine. Thanks for askin'." Big John turned back to the wheel and followed the truck in front of him.

Ace Brinlee drove his purple Pontiac GTO on one of the old hunter's roads in the direction of the Lounge. He knew the Roads End caravan would stop there and the hunters would be given their hunting block location for the day. He had Leon Barrett and pure meanness on his evil mind and nothing was going to turn him from his premeditated action against the ex-Georgia Bulldog and any of the other Roads End members that might have the misfortune to cross his black hearted path. Ace knew the same shortcut Leon knew and he had no one to suggest he didn't take it. Ace turned the GTO toward the always interesting No-Go Road on the very day you shouldn't go that way. Ace Brinlee hadn't had such a good Friday night and it looked like his Saturday morning wasn't going to be any better as he headed toward the slick wet red Georgia clay of No-Go Road. He must of not known why it was called that. In spite of all its mechanical prowess, the GTO was not much of an off road vehicle.

The caravan of hunter's vehicles was easing down All Night Road on the way to the first drive of the new season. Leon Barrett stopped the lead truck when the horn of the second truck in line sounded behind him, stopping the forward movement of all the other vehicles. They were just South of the Clay Hill. Paul Peavey jumped out of the second truck and eyeballed the grass by the roadside trying to spot a huge diamondback rattlesnake he had seen slither across the road and vanish into the high weeds. Paul Peavey Jr., a young man in his early twenties, joined his father and moved slowly into the high grass. He was feeling braver than the others because he was wearing his calf high Gokey boots.

About fifteen of the other hunters had left their trucks to watch the snake hunt from the safety of the high level road. As one of the safe spectators, Bill Wood, took one of his shotgun shells out of his pocket and threw it at Paul Jr., hitting his Carhart overalls about shin high. When the shell hit the target it sounded like a loud slap of hands against the canvas leg and boot. Paul Jr., just knew the big snake had struck him from his hiding place in the grass. In two long and fearful jumps he was back on the road standing with the spectators, inspecting his imaginary wound, as the others exploded with foolish laughter. Paul Jr. knew the joke was on him, but don't tell his pounding heart it wasn't the snake.

The spectators got back into their vehicles and Leon led the way to Jim Mott's Lounge. The veteran hunters all knew the sudden heavy rain the night before could very well cause the diamondback devils to start crawling in all directions, looking for high and dry ground. Paul Peavey was back in the truck with his father, but he was not very happy with the scary joke that had been played on him. The caravan continued toward the destination where Leon

The Huntmaster

Barrett, the huntmaster of the day, would assign stands to the hunting groups. The Lounge was only a half mile away.

Ace Brinlee was struggling to keep his purple Pontiac GTO in the middle of No-Go Road. Even after he had slowed his speed to a mile an hour the wet slick clay was in charge of where the GTO would move. Ace knew he was in trouble and he may never get to his destination at all. He stopped the car, but it kept moving as the slippery clay caused the car to slide along. Ace pulled the emergency break as hard as he could and turned the steering wheel so the tires would turn inward and dig into the thick red clay. The GTO stopped moving forward. Ace Brinlee was stranded three miles from the Lounge and the huntmaster, Leon Barrett. The evil one was on the verge of a serious and total nervous and mental breakdown. He was definitely on the edge within himself and on the edge of No-Go Road.

All the hunting vehicles were parked all over the area called the Lounge. Leon Barrett leaned against the hood of Don Stover's red Bug Blaster pest control truck and called out the hunting block assignments for the first day of the hunt. He had nine segments of wooded land to distribute among the more than ready hunters. He started with Bill Wood.

"Bill, you take number three today." Bill nodded his head and walked toward his red Bronco where his son, John, and Hugh Powell were waiting to take to the woods. Leon continued the assignments as Bill walked away. John and Hugh were waiting in the truck. Bill knew they were ready to hunt. They had waited long enough. He looked at Hugh Powell.

"We'll have the poacher's tree stand at number three. That's a good spot. You'll like it out there. Let's roll." Bill climbed into the driver's side of his truck and the hunters were off to the poacher's tree stand at block number three. Leon had more assignments.

"Mister Luther, y'all cover block number seven." Luther Reynolds smiled.

"It don't matter where you put us, we're gonna beat all you pissbirds. We're gonna be the meatpackers today." He looked at Raymond Lloyd, the real Meatpacker and smiled. Raymond nodded respectfully to his elder and smiled back. The green monster Jeep with Dallas Thomas, James Reynolds, Leonard Hooks and the driver, Luther Reynolds, was headed for number seven. Leon turned to Jimmy Carter.

"Jimmy, y'all take the railroad side of number three." Jimmy nodded and walked away to his truck where his family members waited. Leon continued the roll call.

Ace Brinlee looked back at his GTO that was stuck in the sopping wet red Georgia clay of No-Go Road. He walked slowly for fear he would slip and fall into the wet clay. His boots were covered with the clay and the bottom of both legs of his dungarees were covered too. He held his high powered rifle over his shoulder. He was in search of Leon Barrett and the Roads End hunters.

After Leon had assigned all the opening day hunting positions he gave his hunting group the "beehive" stand. Big John Blanyer's group was headed to the Shingle Mill tree stand while Raymond Lloyd's group was headed to his favorite spot known as the short six. All the hunting vehicles were on the move and the hunt had officially begun. The vehicles splashed through mud puddles on the way to the blocks and tree stands. The ground was saturated with water and was soft under foot. Nothing, however, would stop the opening day of the hunt. It was going to be the most exciting and unusual day in the history of Roads End.

Bill Wood dropped his thirteen year old son, John, off at the dead end of Rosier Road near block number three. He left a stool for John to sit on while he was waiting for the dogs to make a run. Bill and Hugh Powell settled into the block. Hugh climbed up into the "poacher's" tree stand at Bill's polite invitation. Bill was experimenting with a new and comfortable approach to the waiting game of hunting. He had installed brackets on the roof of his Bronco and he attached a fiberglass swivel chair to the brackets, giving him a high perch above as he waited. Bill sat back in his new contraption with his gun across his lap and talked out loud to himself.

"Alright Bullet. Just run 'em past me, boy. I'll pick 'em off from here." He knew that Bronco Bill's beagles were in search of a big buck to run him to block three and into the sights of Bronco Bill, himself.

The first buck of the day was jumped by Raymond Lloyd's dog, Mirth, off the short six, where Raymond was waiting. It was a beautiful nine pointer and it went down with a single clean shot. Raymond didn't miss very often. In fact, he never missed. He was, no doubt, the best marksman of all the members at Roads End. He was the "Meatpacker".

Ace Brinlee looked up at the fire tower and he could see the Sand Hill on the other side. He knew he was near the Roads End boundaries and he didn't want anyone to see him on foot and in the predicament he had found for himself. He would stay on the road, but take to the woods if he saw anyone approaching. He took a few steps and stopped dead in his tracks as he watched the biggest rattlesnake he had ever seen cross the road in front of him. Ace shouldered his gun and was going to shoot the monster reptile, but he thought about the noise he would make with the shot and he knew it would bring the Roads End posse to investigate the situation. He didn't need that so he allowed the eight feet of slithering muscle and sure death to go about its business. He was careful as he continued on the road, knowing where there was one snake, there was most likely more.

The word went out over the radios that Meatpacker had packed the first buck of the new season. No one was surprised by the news, but they were all a bit envious of the expert hunter and his ability to pack in the deer meat.

Bill Wood's eyes widened and he sat up straight in his fiberglass swivel chair when he heard two shots ring out. He looked in the direction of the shots and knew his son, John, had fired his gun. As Bill climbed down off his new perch on top of his red Bronco, a voice came over his radio. He recognized the voice belonging to his fellow Roads End member, Cliff Weldon.

"Come on down here, Bill. Let's see if we can track down this deer your boy took a shot at." Bill didn't even think about his guest, Hugh, as he jumped into his Bronco and raced to where he had left John earlier.

At number seven, James Reynolds was in a battle with a six foot long rattlesnake. James never used his gun on the snakes that crossed his path. He had no problem killing them he just would not shoot them. He enjoyed the manly art of hand to fang combat.

James had a two prong forked gig pole in his hand. It was his weapon of choice for the big six footer. The huge snake was striking forward and pulling back as James would thrust the pole forward and pull it back. The snake jumped forward and James jumped back. The snake coiled back and James moved forward. From a safe distance Dallas Thomas had a question and a suggestion for the rather busy James Reynolds.

"Are you crazy? Back away and I'll blow him to pieces." Dallas shouldered a shotgun and aimed both barrels at the moving snake. James kept his concentration and eyes on the mad and aggressive reptile.

"No, don't. I got 'em." James jumped back as the snake actually struck out, sinking its fangs into James' knee high boots. Leonard Hooks had left the area and gone into the woods on his own, but Luther Reynolds was still with Dallas Thomas as they both watched James battle with the beast.

"Let the crazy bastard be, Dallas. He thinks he's a damn mongoose." James smiled at Luther's advice for Dallas, as he thrust the gig pole one last time. The double prongs stuck deep into the spade shaped head of the huge and dangerous diamondback, pinning it to the ground. The body of the snake twisted and turned, trying to pull its head free. James gripped the pole and pushed its metal prongs deeper into the head of the snake and into the ground.

"I told ya I had 'em. I've been fightin' these devils since I was a boy. I wanted to see if I still had it." James knelt down next to thrashing snake. Took out his big hunting knife and cut the moving body away from the pinned head. James looked up at Dallas.

"Luther's right, ya know. I am a mongoose."

Ace Brinlee had seen one near the canal by the catfish pond tram. Paul Peavey had stopped the caravan for one on the All Night Road. James Reynolds had killed a six footer. None of the hunters realized it yet, but the rattlesnakes of Roads End were on the move and had joined the hunt.

Bill Wood stopped his red chair topped, Bronco on the road and stepped out of the vehicle. He saw John near a big tree with his head down in disgust. John's soft-rimmed hat was on the ground a few feet away from him. Bill knew he had thrown his hat as part of his disappointment. John looked up as his father walked toward him. He shook his head.

"Dad, I missed him. I shot right at his head and I missed him. He just kept running." Bill put his arm around John's thirteen year old shoulders.

"We've all missed one before, son."

"I know. I just don't know how I missed him. It was a buck too. I saw his horns."

Cliff Weldon drove up and had Lolly, one of Bill's dogs with him. Bill turned to the two new arrivals.

"He missed him, Cliff." Cliff smiled.

"I don't think so, Bill. I feel it was a good hit. Ya know how

Six Footer

sometimes ya just have a feelin'? Let's take Lolly out there and try to find him." Bill looked down at Lolly.

"Cliff, you know Lolly's only claim to fame is being an escape artist. There's no pen made by man that can hold her. But, she can't hunt worth a damn." Cliff smiled and touched the dog on the head.

"Come on, Lolly, let's show your daddy here, you can find that buck." Bill and John followed Cliff and Lolly into the woods.

Jimmy Carter and Jimbo were sitting together in the woods. Jimmy was sitting on a tree stump and Jimbo straddled a log. Jimmy looked at his son as Jimbo yawned like a wide mouth frog.

"You all right, boy?" Jimbo nodded.

"Yes, sir."

"You boys can't stay up all night talkin' and laughin' if you're gonna hunt early."

"Dad, we're sleepin' in the same room with the Fatman." Jimmy smiled because he understood what Jimbo meant. They were silent for a moment.

Donny Carter was climbing down from his tree stand only a few yards from where the other two Carters were sitting. As his right foot made contact with, what he thought was the ground, the ground moved underneath his foot. Donny pushed his foot down, but got no traction at all. He slipped and found himself belly down on the ground face-to-face with a huge rattlesnake. Another six footer. The reptile was just passing through, but after it felt Donny's heavy boot the thick snake was coiled and ready to strike. Donny Carter was as scared as he had ever been. He knew he had to be still and calm, but he also knew he couldn't have a staring contest with the devil very long. He would lose that contest.

The huge snake was drawn back like a spring ready to jump forward. Its six rattles, one button tail stood straight up pointing to the sky and then started shaking, like a baby's rattle, warning

Donny that the confrontation was near and that he was in grave danger. Donny saw movement above him and a flash of light as the snake jumped forward, extending its body toward Donny's head. At the same time the snake jumped, Donny rolled to his side, hoping the snake would miss him and not follow his movement. He rolled his body over a number of times, then looked back for the snake. When Donny focused his eyes on the snake, he saw that the huge snake was in two three-foot pieces. Both pieces were squirming and thrashing on the wet ground. Donny looked up and smiled. The movement and the flash he had seen above him was his brother, Jimmy, swinging a jungle machete down on the body of the extended snake and the flash was the sun reflecting off the blade of the big knife. Donny rolled over on his back and looked up into the tree stand above him.

"What the hell took ya so long?"

Cliff Weldon followed Lolly, the escape artist, while Bill and John walked the edge of the road. Bill could see John's disappointment and he was sure they were wasting their hunting time, looking for a deer that was long gone and still running. Bill put his arm around John's shoulder to console him one last time before they went back to the other side of the road and set up again. John looked up at his father, but could not manage even a little smile. Cliff Weldon's voice came from about fifty yards away. They could only hear him. They could not see him in the tall grass.

"Bill, over here! Looks to me like that boy of yours has killed himself a, one. . . two. . . three. . . four. . . five. . . six. . . seven. . . eight, an eight point buck."

Jimbo cut the rattles off the tail end of the dead snake. He put them into his pocket to show the others later. The sound of a dog yelping turned the three Carters toward the woods on the other side of the road. Jimmy's heart raced in his chest and his blood flow changed directions in his veins. He had heard that painful cry from a dog before. He knew the dog was hurt and he knew in his gut another rattlesnake had caused the pain. He turned to Donny and Jimbo.

"No use in going in there. We'll be screamin' too if we try to find that dog. If he comes out we'll try to save him, but goin' in there will just put us all in danger. I knew that rain last night would get those devils on the move. It's too wet for 'em to stay put. They've gotta move to dry ground. I hate the poisonous bastards."

Jimbo Carter looked past his father and saw one of their dogs walk slowly out of the high grass onto the road. The dog staggered for a few steps and fell over on its side.

"Daddy, look!" Jimmy and Donny both looked in the same direction Jimbo indicated and saw the dog lying on the side of the dirt road. Jimmy hurried to the wounded animal.

"It's Joe. Damn them fanged devils. They're after us again." Donny and Jimbo joined Jimmy at the dog's side. Three more of their dogs, No-name, J. C. and Rooster, walked out of the high grass and stood near them on the road.

Leon Barrett whistled for his pit bull, Bud Bo. He saw the dog once earlier for a few seconds as he crossed the road to Leon's left, then the dog was gone. Ed Barrett was sitting in an old rusty metal folding chair, someone had left in the woods near the beehive stand. His brother, Ramsey, had taken the high position in the tree stand. Leon knew Bud Bo was near the train tracks and he wanted to get the dog back with them before the train came through. There had been no trains yet that morning so Leon knew one was due, if the usual schedules held true. Bud Bo was not listening because he didn't come in when Leon gave the signal. Leon heard the noise of an engine and he turned to see who was coming. It was Doc Johnson. He was alone in his medicine man wagon. Doc stopped the truck next to Leon. He stuck his head out the window.

"Jimmy's got a dog down. Rattler got 'em. Did ya hear it." Leon shook his head.

"Somethin's wrong with my radio. We been deaf most of the day."

"Jimmy says he's dead. I'm goin' out there to see about it, but I'm sure Jimmy's right. He's seen enough dead dogs lately." Leon shook his head. He knew how Jimmy Carter felt about his dogs and how he took care of them like they were his children. They had spoken about such tragedies that very morning and, now, one had occurred. Leon waved Doc on and the medicine man started to pull away slowly. He looked back at a sad Leon Barrett.

"Oh, by the way, Butch. Meatpacker dropped the first one and the Wood boy, John, dropped the second one. In other words, two deer, one dog." Doc nodded to Leon and his truck moved away on down the road. Cliff Weldon drove away down Rosier Road and left Bill and John with their moment of family glory and excitement. Bill put Lolly into the back seat of the Bronco.

"You did a good job, girl." Bill joined John in the road where they had placed John's first kill. Bill got his camera from the front seat of the Bronco and was ready to record a moment of family hunting history. To say who was the most proud, John or his father could be debated until the end of time with no clear cut resolution to the question.

Bill told John to kneel down on one knee behind the deer, lift it's head and hold his gun up over the head and use the horns as a gun rack. John had his hat back on his head as he posed with the beautiful, white bellied eight pointer. It was a great opening day. It was a great birthday. It was a great picture.

Tom Cravey walked out of the woods at number three holding two dead rattlesnakes, one in each hand. Their deadly heads were gone. He held them up at shoulder level and they both still touched the ground below. Hugh Powell looked down from the tree stand.

"Found some company out there, did ya?" Tom dropped the heavy snakes to the ground.

"They went by me, one on each side. I thought for a second I was a goner. I don't know why, but I stomped on the big one's head and held him down 'til I could cut his head off. I thought I'd better chase the other one down before he got to one of the dogs or somebody else. I was lucky with him too. I grabbed him below the head before he got me." Hugh climbed down from the stand to see the monster snakes. Tom looked around the area.

"Where's Bill?" Hugh stepped off the last board on the stand.

"He went to John's spot. The boy fired twice. Bill wanted to be sure he was all right. Look at the size of those bastards."

Ace Brinlee walked onto the concrete slab outside the front door of the Roads End lodge. His boots and clothes were covered with the dried red Georgia clay from his encounter with No-Go Road. It was obvious he had fallen a number of times during his adventure and the clay was splattered on his face and caked in his hair. Even his rifle was covered with the red clay. It looked as if the barrel of the gun was clogged with the clay also, like he had fallen and stuck the end of the gun into the clay. Only Ace Brinlee would know how many times he had slipped and fallen during his walk on No-Go Road. Ace walked to the far right side of the building where a hand lever, big lipped water pump stood tall next to a fifty five gallon drum of rain water that was filled to the top edge. He propped the clay covered gun up against the outside wall of the building.

Ace stuck his clay coated face and head into the cold rain water, overflowing the drum onto the ground at his feet. The water took the thick granular clay off his face instantly, leaving the clay to settle in the bottom of the rain barrel. Ace threw his head back and shook his head like a dog shaking water off its body, splashing the water into the air behind him. He then stuck one arm into the cold water washing away the clay and then the other arm, leaving more clay to settle on the bottom of the rain barrel.

Ace began splashing the water out of the barrel onto his clothes and the rest of his clay covered body. He heard a noise behind him and he reached for the clay coated rifle.

"Now, I hope you ain't gonna fire that cannon anywhere close by. You do know it's gonna explode and kill you and anyone else in the immediate vicinity." Ace had to turn around to face his old friend and Friday night nemesis, Don "the cook" Crawford. Don was once again holding up his double barreled scatter gun he had held on Ace the night before. It was pointed at Ace's wet head. Don couldn't resist.

"Damn, boy. I feel like I've been here before. You know what I mean, don't ya. They call 'em day-za-voots or somethin' like that. I think it's from France."

Ace Brinlee wasn't listening to Don's foolish chatter. He still held his rifle in his hand, but after Don's warning he knew he wasn't going to use the disabled weapon. Ace put the gun back against the side of the building. Don smiled.

"Smart move there, Ace. Looks like you've been out on No-Go. And you bein' on foot, I'd say that hot-rod of yours is out of commission 'til that sun hardens that sweet clay out there." Ace hated the fact the fat little cook was right and was taking the moment to make fun of Ace's situation. He also hated the fact that Don had gotten the drop on him again. Ace couldn't handle two more circle marks on his forehead. He would surely have a mental breakdown if he was humiliated like that again. Ace had to humble himself, but he hated it.

"I don't want no trouble. I had to get that clay off me. I need to call my brother, Buford, and get him out here. Y'all got any phone lines or radios hooked up in there?" Don smiled.

"Can't use 'em. Members only." Ace's face went blood red. Don's face didn't change. He held the shotgun to his shoulder. "Now, get on outside the gate. I'll get in touch with Buford and tell him you're waitin' on Hayner Road where the tracks cross." Ace's face was still red and he raised his voice.

"Hayner! That's at least three miles from here."

"More like four, I'd say." Ace was boiling inside as he looked down the two barrels of Don's shotgun.

"Tell Buford I'm at the gate. I'll stay outside the gate."

"You got no say-so, here. You need to realize who's in charge and who ain't. He 'll be lookin' for you on Hayner. It's your choice if he finds you there or not. That's what life's all about, Ace, makin' good choices." Ace hated the fact he had to listen to a philosophical moment with the fat little cook at Roads End. Don motioned with the barrel of the gun for Ace to move along. The conversation was over.

Ace picked up his rifle and walked off the concrete slab toward the main front gate. Don stood on the slab until Ace was standing outside the gate. Ace was too tired and mad to say anything, but if evil thoughts could kill, Don Crawford would have dropped dead on the spot. He went back into the building. He would call Buford Brinlee and tell him where to find his clay coated, older, but smaller brother, Ace. Ramsey Barrett yelled down to his father from his perch on top of the beehive tree stand.

"Daddy, I can see Bud Bo over by the tracks. He's sniffin' around all over." Leon looked up at Ramsey.

"How far away?" Ramsey looked at Bud Bo and squinted his eyes trying to judge the distance.

"I don't know, Daddy." Leon hurried up the side of the tree stand and stood with Ramsey. Ramsey pointed .

"See? There he is." Leon focused his eyes on the dog. Bud Bo was actually walking on the cross wooden slats of the tracks. Leon knew the possible danger.

"He's only about a quarter mile away. He needs to get off that track. If he keeps walkin' though, he'll walk up to us, right here. Wouldn't that be a hoot?" Ramsey smiled at the word, hoot. Leon climbed back down from the tree stand where Ed was standing.

"You want me to go get the dog, Dad?" Leon smiled at his oldest.

"You don't mind, son? You'll meet up with him if he stays near the tracks. He's comin' this way, anyway. Thanks, Ed." Ed nodded and left the woods for the road and then left the road for the train tracks. His brother yelled from high in the tree stand.

"He's still comin' this way, Ed. Just stay on the tracks and he'll walk right into your arms." Ed raised his hand to Ramsey, but he didn't look back. Leon sat up against a tree near the stand and cleaned the mud off the bottom of his boots with a stick. His heart jumped in his big chest when he heard the sound he had not heard all day. No one liked that sound when the hunt was on and the dogs were out running. It was the whistle of an approaching Seaboard Coast Line train and it would pass the beehive stand in a matter of minutes. The whistle sounded more like a woman screaming to get out of her way, or face the punishment. Ramsey's eyes widened when he looked in the direction of the whistle and saw the train headed their way. Leon stood up and yelled up at Ramsey.

"Can you see it, son?" Ramsey's heart raced in his little chest.

"Yes, sir. I can."

"How far away is it?" Ramsey took a deep breath and squinted his eyes again. Not because he couldn't see, but because he was trying the judge the distance again. Ramsey looked down at his concerned father.

"I don't know, Daddy. I'm sorry."

"Can you see the dog?" Ramsey looked out again.

"Yes, sir. He's still comin'."

"Is he still on the track?"

"Yes, sir. Right in the middle. He's sniffin' and walkin'." The train whistle sounded again. Ed tried to see it through the trees, but it had not turned the bend yet. Ramsey yelled with fear in his young voice.

"Daddy, the train's almost to Bud Bo. I can see 'em both." The whistle blew again and then again. Leon knew the engineer was trying to blow the dog off the tracks. Leon also knew that in most cases the dogs would not jump off the tracks and would try to outrun the faster train, like Jimmy Carter had said earlier that morning. Ramsey yelled again.

"He's runnin', Daddy! He's running fast! He's turnin' the bend, right now! I can see him comin' right at us!" Leon ran out to the road and then crossed to the tracks. He couldn't see Ed, the dog, or the train from where he was standing. Ramsey's position above had given him the advantage. The whistle sounded again. Leon knew Bud Bo was in big trouble.

Ed could see Bud Bo running right toward him as he stood about ten yards off the track. Ed clapped his hands and yelled to the dog, trying to call the scared dog off the tracks. Ed looked behind the dog and saw that the train was only about thirty yards away and closing fast. Bud Bo did not even look toward Ed as he ran past him. The train shot past Ed and he knew the train would catch the dog in a matter of seconds. The speed of the train stirred up sand and leaves into the air, causing Ed to cover his eyes and move away from the tracks for his own safety.

Leon could see Bud Bo running toward him now. The front of the train engine was only ten yards away from the fleeing dog. Leon had to try.

"Come on, boy! Come to me, boy! That's it, run!" Leon clapped his hands too. Bud Bo was about twenty yards from Leon when the front of the huge train overtook the tired pit bull and gobbled him up like he was a mere appetizer for the big machine. The engine went by Leon and blew sand and leaves into the air again. Leon covered his face like Ed had to do. He closed his eyes for a second and heard Ramsey scream from above.

"Daddy, look!" Leon turned back to the track and focused his eyes on the other cars as they passed by him. He could see what Ramsey was screaming about. Bud Bo was under the cars being bounced around like a rubber ball. The engine was pulling twenty-two cars and a dirty faded red caboose. Bud Bo was hit and bounced by every one of the cars. The three Barrett's watched in horror as their favorite dog was pounded unmercifully. It seemed as if the dog tumbled in one place on the track. He just kept rolling and bouncing, hitting the tracks and the underside of the moving cars. It was only appropriate that the caboose passed over him last. Dallas Thomas made a welcomed call over his radio.

"Any great white hunter, interested in a cold can of Schlitz beer and a bag of boiled peanuts should make tracks to the Lounge. It's time for a break. Bring your lies with ya." Everyone heard Dallas' information except Leon and he boys.

Bud Bo's limp and battered body lay in the middle of the tracks. All three Barretts stood over the rag doll dog. Leon knelt down on one knee and touched his dog's side. Leon's eyes opened wide.

"He's still breathin', boys!. He's still alive! Ed get the truck!" Ed didn't hesitate. He wanted to save the dog, but he also wanted to drive the truck. "Ramsey, when Ed gets here, get the army blanket from behind the seat." Leon stroked his unconscious friend.

"You hold on, boy. We're gonna get you to Doc. You just keep breathin'." Leon didn't want to do much to the dog until Doc got a look at him. The dog was out cold, but Leon didn't see any broken legs or any blood, for that matter. He knew the injuries had to be internal and he knew the dog would most likely die. Just the fact that the tough little pit bull was still breathing made Leon try. He figured if Bud Bo had gone through what Leon had witnessed and he was still hanging on to life, Leon needed to join the dog's courageous battle. That's the kind of thoughts real men have.

Ed drove the truck up on the road next to the track. Ramsey took the blanket out of the front seat and carried it to his father. Leon wrapped the limp dog in the blanket and picked it up like it was a baby in his big strong arms. Leon moved to the passenger's side of the truck and moved slowly to sit down with the dog cradled in his arms. Ramsey jumped into the back bed of the truck to give his father more room in the cab. Ed hit the gas peddle.

The Lounge was alive with movement, activity and thirsty hunters. Dallas' call over the radio waves had brought most of the hunters into the area where they had carried out their ritual the night before and the huntmaster had given them their hunting positions earlier that morning. The rolling stock of trucks and Jeeps were parked side-by-side, surrounding the Lounge and forming a closed fortress of steel and rubber.

Dallas Thomas and Leonard Hooks were handing out cold cans of Schlitz beer from the back of one of the trucks, while Luther Reynolds was trying to sell bags of boiled peanuts to the beer drinkers. Nobody was buying because they knew Luther was going to give them a bag, sooner or later.

The big rattlesnakes were everywhere. James Reynolds was walking around with a can of beer in one hand and the huge rattlesnake he had killed in his other hand. Tom Cravey had his two snakes draped over each shoulder as if they were part of his jungle attire. It was obvious he considered himself quite fashionable for the occasion. At one time, as he moved through the other hunters, he held one of the snakes between his legs and asked the question, "Who's the Meatpacker, now." It was a good laugh.

Donny Carter was carrying his dead snake around, too. The fact his snake had been cut into two pieces didn't hamper Donny's effort to show it to the others. Donny had put the big snake back together using three inch wide silver duct tape he took from Raymond Lloyd's tool box. Meatpacker's truck was parked at the Lounge, but he didn't drive it there. The Fatman, Haystacks, was hunting with Raymond and when he heard Dallas' call for beer and food he had to come on in. His rumbling huge belly gave him no choice. Raymond Lloyd stayed in the woods for another run. He was a true hunter. He was the best. He was the Meatpacker.

It was bad for the huntmaster to have a broken radio. He didn't hear the call that went out from Dallas Thomas for a social hour at the Lounge. He also didn't hear Doc Johnson's call to bring any medical problems to the Lounge so he could attend to the hunters and the dogs. Doc knew he couldn't save the deer or the snakes. The medicine man had his office set up on the back of his truck. Jimmy Carter was sitting on the ground near Doc's truck next to a blanket that covered his fatally bitten dog, Joe. Doc was putting a bandage on another dog that had gotten his leg caught on a fence wire near the power lines.

It was just a fortunate and calculated coincidence that Leon had directed Ed to drive to the Lounge. Leon knew it was about the time of day when most of the hunters were ready for a break from the quiet waiting. They needed to talk loud, tell a few tales, drink a few beers and eat a snack. Leon was hoping Doc would be there, too. He would be right. Ed pressed the gas peddle down harder.

James Reynolds walked by Donny Carter holding his huge dead snake. He stopped and stared at Donny's attempt to use the silver tape to mend his severed reptile. Donny looked up at the old

NO GO RD.
UNION CAMP–PRIVATE RD.

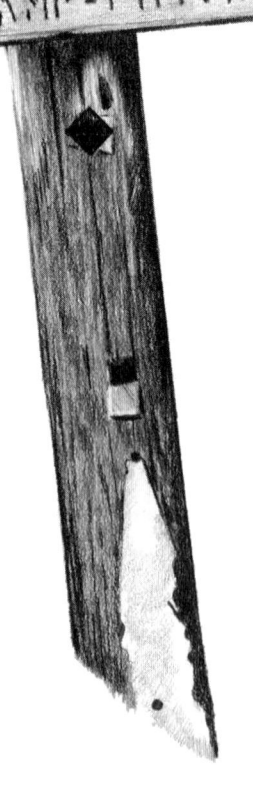

snake fighter and shrugged his shoulders. James shook his head and walked away. Sometimes there are just no appropriate words.

Ace Brinlee was about a half mile from the Hayner Road crossing when he saw his brother's Black Ford Cyclone GT coming toward him. Ace was relieved at the sight of the car and he realized his ordeal on foot would soon be over. Buford stopped the car with the driver's side next to his tired and filthy older brother. Buford rolled down the window.

"What the hell happened to you. You look awful. Ya hurt?" Ace was on the edge. His frustration level was as high as ever and the fact he was fatigued only added to his poor mental state. Ace stared at his younger, but bigger, brother.

"Just get me home. I gotta get this crap off of me." Buford stepped out of the car.

"Let me get something out of the trunk for you to sit on. I just put those new Fingerhut covers on my seats. I've got towels in the trunk." Buford moved to the trunk and opened it. Ace walked over to the trunk also and threw his clay covered and barrel-clogged rifle into the trunk. Buford pulled a big sheet from the trunk.

"I forgot I had this old paintin' sheet. Here use this." Buford handed Ace the paint speckled sheet. Ace walked to the passenger's side of the car, opened the door, put the sheet over the seat and sat down. Buford looked at the clay covered gun, then closed the trunk and joined Ace in the car.

"Where's your car?" Ace lay his head back on the seat.

"We can't get to it. It's on No-Go. The clay's too wet. No sense tryin' 'til it dries up out there." Buford couldn't help himself.

"Why would you go out to No-Go after that rain storm?" Ace's face went red.

"I just made a mistake, dammit. Can ya let it be? Just take me home." Buford still couldn't help it.

"How did that fat cook out there find out about where you

were? I thought you were gonna stay away from there." Ace hated to talk about it, but he knew Buford would not stop.

"I tried to get this crap off me. I wanted to use the phone to call you. The little bastard held a gun on me and he made me leave. He said he'd call you. I had to walk from there to here. I'm gonna fix that little shit. I promise. Now, leave me alone and get me home. I gotta take a shower." Buford started the Cyclone and pushed the shift into gear, turned the car around and headed back up the road. He would drive, but he would wait for Ace to start any more conversation. Buford knew the rest of the ride to Ace's trailer would be a quiet one. The black Ford Cyclone GT was on the move.

Ed Barrett drove his father's truck into the Lounge area and stopped next to Luther Reynolds' green monster. Ramsey jumped out of the truck bed and opened the door for his father and Bud Bo. Most of the hunters had turned to see the truck when it pulled in. They moved toward Leon when they saw the urgency in his movement and the bundle he was carrying so gently. Big John Blanyer was the first to meet him.

"Butch, what is it?" Leon didn't stop. Big John moved with him as other men stepped up.

"It's my dog. The train hit 'em. He's still alive. Is Doc here?" A single voice hollered from the crowd.

"Doc's over by the paok tree." Leon knew where the poak tree was and he moved quickly in that direction, with the others following behind him. Ed and Ramsey followed too.

The poak tree was an unusual freak of the woods. It was actually a straight up pine tree with a live oak wrapped around it in some way. The bark of both trees had been fused together in time and it looked like one tree. It had been used as a prank many times when someone would point it out to a newcomer or guest would be told how the great pine had grown into an oak. They would be told about the poak tree being indigenous only to the Southeast

Georgia counties, such as Glynn, Charlton and Camden. Some visitors still look for the poak orchard that allegedly is somewhere near the number five block.

Doc turned to see what the noise and confusion was behind him. He saw Leon Barrett with the blanket held close to his chest. Doc met Leon at the tailgate of his truck.

"Doc, it's Bud Bo. The train hit him. He's still breathin'. I can't believe it, but he is." Leon lay the dog gently in the bed of the truck and opened the army blanket. He stepped back from his friend and let Doc go to work. There was very little talk from the other hunters. Ramsey Barrett was standing near his father. He turned his head to his left as someone moved up next to him. It was Tom Cravey wanting to see what was going on at Doc's truck. Ramsey's heart jumped in his little chest again when he saw the two big rattlesnakes draped across both of Tom's shoulders. Tom smiled at Ramsey, puckered his lips up like he was going to kiss the boy, and shook the rattles on the snake's tail at Ramsey. Ramsey gave a half grin and moved away from Tom's two snakes and puckered lips. Tom Cravey was a true lady's man, with his tan skin, black curly hair, and muscular, hard as a knot, body. He always teased the young boys about kissing them on the cheek as his official greeting when they first came to Roads End. Most of the boys stayed clear of his style of greeting.

Almost every hunter was gathered around the back of Doc's clinic on wheels. They all knew how important Bud Bo was to Leon and his boys. Bud Bo's lifeless body lay on the dark green army blanket. The dog's eyes were half open and glazed over. Doc touched the dog all over its body. He pushed on its ribs, checked it's legs, and listened to its heart with a stethoscope. Doc turned to the concerned and anxious Leon Barrett.

"This dog's just unconscious. He's out, cold, but he's got no broken bones, no cuts and I don't think he's got any serious injuries on the inside. He's just out. That's all I can say. He may come around. He may not. The unconscious state tells me it's a head injury, but I can't judge how serious it is. Him being out and all makes it serious." Leon didn't know what to say. He wanted to tell Doc what he and his sons had witnessed. It would surely be one of the wild stories told at the Lounge. Doc interrupted Leon's thoughts.

"It's unusual for anyone or anything to be hit by a train and not have more visible damage than this. Are you sure the dog was hit by the train or did y'all just find him near the tracks?" Leon looked at Ramsey, then at Ed. Then back at Doc.

"You ain't heard the half of it, Doc. I don't know how to say it, but to just say it. I know how crazy it's gonna sound, but here goes." Everyone standing near the truck became quiet.

"He tried to outrun the train. We saw the whole thing. We tried to call him off the tracks, but he was too scared. The engineer tried to blow the horn to get him off at least five times, maybe more. But, ol' Bud Bo just kept on runnin' straight ahead." A lone voice hollered from the crowd.

"They'll do that, ya know. I've seen 'em do it myself." Leon continued.

"When the train caught him, he went under the engine, like it ate him. Then it got crazy. Ramsey yelled to me when he saw it." The men were as quiet as they would be the entire time at the Lounge as Leon told his true, but unbelievable story.

"Every car being pulled by that engine hit that dog. He bounced around under the cars like a stuffed animal. He actually stayed in one spot on the tracks as he bounced off the cross bars and up to the bottom of each car. There was at least twenty cars of that train and each one hit him. We thought he was torn to pieces, but here he is. Y'all see him. The tough little bastard's still breathin'." The crowd started mumbling about what they had just been told. Doc had a suggestion.

"All we can do is wait and see if he wakes up. Leave him here on the blanket. He can stay covered and warm. Time will tell us."

Tom Cravey lay his two snakes on the ground side-by-side. One was about four inches longer than the other one. James Reynolds lay his snake down on the ground right next to Tom's longest. James smiled and looked at Tom.

"That's three big ass killers layin' there, ain't it?" Tom nodded.

"Damn, James. Yours is almost a foot longer than my big one. That's a hell-of-a snake." James nodded, too.

"I think there's a shit load of these devils still out there. I ain't too crazy 'bout walkin' 'round out there with the daddy of these three slimy bastards waitin' on me. It hampers our ability to hunt." Donny Carter stepped up next to James.

"It's that heavy rain last night. They 'bout run us off three years ago after a rain." Donny lay his monster snake on the ground next to the other three snakes. It was about three inches longer than James' snake. Tom had to say something to James.

"Holy shit, James. Donny's is bigger than yours." James had a question and an answer.

"How the hell do you expect to count a damn snake that's been taped together. Hell boy, it ain't got no head or rattles. It might be two little snakes taped together to make one big snake, as far as we know. You gotta disqualify ya'self from the contest. It's the only right thing to do." All the hunters within listening distance started laughing at James' rationale for Donny's snake not being part of the contest. Donny couldn't let it go.

"I didn't even know it was a damn contest, you crazy ol' fart. I just dropped the snake down there. I thought I could add it to the kill line. You act like there's a damn prize for havin' the biggest." James had Donny going and wasn't even considering letting up on the young man.

"It's the principle of the thing. There's always been a contest on who's got the biggest since the beginning of time. You can't have a man sayin' his is bigger than yours out loud, so forget the damn snakes. Don't make me whip out my own personal boa constrictor and show you yours ain't bigger than mine." They all exploded with laughter at James' change of the subject matter. Donny shook his head at the foolishness and picked up his taped rattlesnake. Donny knew James would whip "it" out to add to the drama. He didn't want to see the old man's manhood, bigger or not. The size issue, snake or wacker, was over.

Leon heard the laughter from his seat on the tailgate of his truck. He could see his Uncle James and he knew he was doing something crazy to someone. Leon smiled, shook his head, and took a drink from a cold Schlitz beer can. Jimmy Carter had something on his mind and he needed to talk to the huntmaster.

"Butch, I'm sorry about Bud Bo." Leon looked at his friend.

"Thank ya, Jimmy. I'm sorry about Joe, too." Jimmy nodded.

"I know it's early, but I ain't too crazy about makin' another run today. I think we need to let these damn snakes settle. There's just too many of 'em. They outnumber us and the dogs. I've seen 'em bad, but never like this." Leon knew Jimmy Carter was right and he was using his usual good judgement for humans and dogs.

"Well, the snakes sent us packin' three years ago and they're even worse today. I'll talk to the others after we all have a little brew and some eats." Jimmy nodded again and moved away to talk to his brother Donny and check on his son, Jimbo.

Meatpacker's first deer was in the back of his truck. He had sent it in with Haystacks for the others to see. Haystacks had left the truck for beer and food and had not even thought about the deer in the back. Tom Cravey walked past the truck and saw the deer.

"I tell ya what. That Meatpacker can take 'em down, can't he?" Lonnie Sikes and Big John Blanyer were standing near by. They all walked to the truck and Tom held the deer's head up so they could see it. The noise from an approaching vehicle made them turn toward the new arrival. The three men couldn't believe their eyes as the Bronco came closer. John's first deer was on the roof of the Bronco strapped into the fiberglass chair and sitting up as if it was taking a sightseeing tour of the area. Bill Wood's red Bronco stopped next to Meatpacker's truck and it would be the last vehicle to complete the fortress around the Lounge. The deer on top was a hilarious sight and the hunters began to move in that direction laughing and pointing at the novelty. The laughter turned to cheers and whistles when John Wood stepped out of the Bronco. They all understood what the first kill meant to the young man. They had all experienced that same day and would always remember the feeling they had too. They crowded around John with hugs, pats on the back, and pleased smiles. The deer was a funny sight sitting straight up in that swivel chair. Bill Wood was definitely in rare form.

The hunters were all looking at John's first deer. It was a great event to have taken place any day, but it was even sweeter when it happened on your birthday. It was the first of many deer John would take down as he grew as a hunter at Roads End, but none would be more remembered and cherished like that first one.

Even though each hunter felt sad about Jimmy Carter's dog, Joe, and Leon's, Bud Bo, they also knew it was a hazard of running the dogs and hunting in general. Dogs had been injured or died before and would as long as the hunts continued. It came with the territory. The atmosphere of the first day remained festive as the empty Schlitz beer cans mounted up. Haystacks was sucking them down like they were those sharp ended white Dixie cups full of water you get from an office cooler. The Fatman had a pile of boiled peanut shells on the ground around him, elephant ankle deep. Jimbo Carter and Little Mac McGehee both looked at the Fatman sitting on the back of Meatpacker's truck. Jimbo stepped closer to Little Mac. He had to speak his mind to his young friend.

"I can't believe he's gonna be sleepin' with us again tonight. Do you know what all those boiled peanuts are gonna do to his stomach? And I heard Mr. Crawford tell my dad he was gonna have a big pot of his special Texas chili ready when we get back. If he adds that chili to those boiled peanuts and we don't change rooms, we're gonna be dead before mornin'. And for God's sake, don't let anyone light a match in there."

The huntmaster, Leon Barrett, stood tall in the back of his truck. Bud Bo was still unconscious and wrapped in the dark green army blanket on the back bed of the truck. Leon put his fingers to his lips and gave his incredibly loud and annoying whistle to get everyone's attention. It never failed. The hunters were looking in his direction.

"Can I get everyone over here, please?" The hunters kept talking and laughing, but a few of them did start walking in the direction of Leon's truck. The talkers soon saw the others moving toward Leon and they followed the movement. They all gathered at the truck and quieted down for the huntmaster.

"Gentlemen, we have a dilemma on our hands today on our first day together, but it wouldn't be Roads End without somethin' crazy goin' on. That's why we love it here. If you're a man ready for excitement, you're in the right place." There were a few mumbles in the crowd until Leon continued talking.

"First, we need to congratulate John Wood again as a group, for his first Roads End kill and his first kill period." They all cheered, whistled and clapped as John and Bill Wood stood there and grinned. Leon went on as the noise died down.

"We'll congratulate Raymond when he gets here, but if you haven't seen it, the first deer of the season's in the back of his truck. As usual he dropped the first one. That sorry bastard." They all laughed as a lone voice yelled from somewhere in the crowd.

Bud Bo

"He is that. He is surely that." They all knew Leon meant no disrespect toward his friend, Meatpacker. Leon had more.

"The dilemma we have is that an army of big, and I mean big, rattlesnakes have invaded our stands. Or, it might be that we have invaded their stands and they don't like us very much." The same single voice yelled, "We don't like them, either." Leon nodded his head.

"That's true. That's very true. The problem is: we have two missing dogs, one dead dog, that we know of, and four of the biggest rattlesnakes I've ever seen in my life, dead, in front of us. We don't know how many others have been spotted or went by us without bein' seen. I don't know how y'all feel about it, but I'm pretty worried about it, myself."

At that moment, Leon stopped talking. He could see his audience was no longer looking at him. They were all looking past him. He saw at least twenty-five sets of eyes widen to their fullest. He turned around to see what they were looking at behind him. Leon's eyes widened like everyone else's.

The dark green army blanket that was wrapped around Bud Bo was moving. There was no noise as the blanket seemed to rise up off the bed of the truck and float in the air, like it was shrouding a ghost. There was more movement and then the blanket fell off both sides of the dog, exposing him to the sunlight and the amazed hunters. Bud Bo stood there on his own four quivering legs, with the dark green army blanket crumpled at his paws.

The spectators were silent as they witnessed a true miracle at the Lounge. Bud Bo made no sound. It looked as though the dog was trying to focus his eyes on the hunters. The dog took two shaky steps forward and stepped out of the blanket. Bud Bo looked up and it was obvious, by the way he wagged his tail, he recognized his friend, Leon Barrett. The miracle dog barked once and the hunters exploded with the loudest and wildest cheer of the day, so far. Leon's heart raced as he picked Bud Bo up into his big arms and held him to his chest. Like the huntmaster had told the other hunters, "You want excitement? Come to Roads End."

Ace Brinlee had both his hands on the wall of his shower as he watched the red clay from No-Go Road fall off his body and wash away down the drain of his bath tub. His ordeal on No-Go and at Roads End was finally over, but he would not forget it anytime soon. It only added to his hatred for Roads End and all who were associated with the hunting camp. As Ace allowed the hot water to run down his back, his unstable mind pounded him with visions of the last twenty-four hours of his uneasy and hateful life.

He first remembered how Leon Barrett pulled him from his car and choked him in front of Molly and his brother, Buford. He thought of how Don Crawford had put that big doubled barreled scatter gun on his forehead and backed him out of the lodge at Roads End. He relived how Leon Barrett chased him and then hit him in the back, knocking him into that cold water filled ditch. His heart pounded in his chest as his anger filled him. Ace hit the wall with his fist when he thought about being thrown through the front door at the Darien truck stop and how Molly treated him and then left him. His last mental flashback was Don Crawford holding that scatter gun on him again and making him walk to Hayner Road. He wanted to kill them all.

Leon Barrett fought back the tears of happiness as he watched his two sons kneeling on the ground petting and touching Bud Bo. It was as if the dog had cheated death. All three Barretts knew what they had seen and by all rites the dog should have been dead. But, there he was, standing upright, tail wagging and enjoying all the attention. Leon looked at Doc Johnson and shook his head. Doc shrugged his shoulders and smiled. Leon climbed back up into the back of his truck. He looked out into the crowd of hunters still standing near the truck.

"Gentlemen, I don't know what's goin' on today. Maybe it's just another day at Roads End, but it has been an interesting morning to say the least." The men were silent once again. "Our dilemma is still with us. Do we make another run and chance losing another dog, or keep manning the stands and lose a hunter? Or do we allow the snakes to find drier ground and settle back into their dens as the sun dries the woods. We have been fortunate up to this point and I, for one, am worried about what will happen next if we stay in the woods with these snakes on the move like they are. Tomorrow is another day to hunt." There was mumbling again from the crowd. "If you want to stay out and finish the day, of course, that's up to you. I know some of you will stay out. Just be careful out there." A single voice came from the crowd.

"Let's stop huntin' and start drinkin'." The hunters exploded with laughter and cheers again. The huntmaster yelled above the wild noises of the Lounge.

"If you make another run, be careful and good luck. If you want some of Don's Texas chili follow me, Ed, Ramsey and Bud Bo to the house."

Truck and Jeep engines started, horns blew and tires started spinning on the dirt, grass and gravel at the Lounge. Haystacks walked to Meatpacker's truck and slowly climbed into the driver's seat. The first kill of the new season was still in the back of the truck. He knew he had to let Raymond know what was happening. He wanted to head to the nearest chili bowl, but he had to take Raymond's truck back. He could only hope Meatpacker would pack it in for the day and go eat chili with the others. Fat chance.

Bill Wood, John and Hugh Powell were in the red Bronco with the empty fiberglass chair on top. John's deer was in the storage area behind the back seat for the ride to the camp. The deer would be hanging on the skinning rack within the hour.

Leon Barrett, Ed, Ramsey and Bud Bo were on their way to the lodge, too. Leon would not allow his boys or his dogs to be in danger as they would be if they returned to the woods that day. He wanted to get Bud Bo into the comfort of the pen so he could keep an eye on the special little pit bull.

Most of the hunting vehicles headed back to the lodge. A few went back into the woods for various reasons. Some would hunt for a few more hours, some would just take a ride and hunt for dogs. Just as fast as the Lounge had filled with rolling stock, it was now empty. Only the peanut shells on the ground gave any indication the Roads End hunters were there.

Chuck "Haystacks" Drew pulled Raymond's truck up to the tree stand at number six. He was hoping Meatpacker was still nearby where he had left him. Haystacks was hungry for that Texas chili waiting for him at the lodge. The seven beers and at least four pounds of boiled peanuts were merely an appetizer for the rotund four hundred plus pounder. He drove slowly on the road looking into the woods where he thought Raymond might be. He listened out the window, but remained in the truck. Getting in and out of anything was a hard chore for him. He only did so if he had to. He would not blow the horn at first, just in case there was a deer around and maybe Raymond had his sights on it right now. The sound of that horn could scare the target. He was hungry, but he knew he wasn't going to blow that horn. Not at the moment, anyway.

Don Crawford was standing over the white stove, stirring two huge boiling pots of his special Texas chili. One, then the other. He looked out the small kitchen window when he heard the sound of horns blowing. Don's eyes popped open wide when he saw the vehicles coming through the main gate. The hunters of Roads End had returned early. He smiled a big one because the chili was ready.

The front yard quickly filled with trucks and Jeeps. Don was happy he would have company. He had been alone most of the morning except for his brief encounter and stand off with his new friend, Ace Brinlee. Don walked to the front door to watch the hunters dismount their rolling stock. He saw James Reynolds first as he was stepping up onto the concrete slab.

"Everybody all right, Mr. James?" James moved to the door.

"Snakes run us off. I'm too old for all this excitement. I never seen 'em so bad before."

"Nobody hurt, I hope." James pressed his lips together.

"Jimmy lost another dog to a rattler. I feel bad about that. Ya never get used to dogs dyin'. Wait'll ya see the dead snakes comin' in. Ya know how to cook 'em, don't ya?" Don wrinkled his forehead.

"I know how, but I don't like to. I'll cook 'em if you want me to."

"Hell no. I just asked ya if ya knew how. You don't have to cook the nasty bastards for me, that's for sure." James walked past Don and went straight to the latrine. The front yard was full of vehicles, excited barking dogs and hungry hunters.

Ace Brinlee stood in front of his bedroom mirror. He tightened his wide belt around the waist of his army issue camouflage pants. The bottom legs of the pants were tucked into the top of his black, lace up, steel toed boots. Ace wore a black tight fitting t-shirt with a small skull and crossbones on one of the short sleeves. The short sleeves squeezed his biceps, making them look even bigger than they were. He slipped a serrated top blade skinning knife into the sheath on his belt. He slipped two smaller knives into two sheaths on the insides of each boot. Ace then strapped a shot gun shell bandolero belt over his right shoulder that went across his chest to the left side of his body.

Ace opened the closet door with the mirror and took out a short handled sawed-off shotgun with a wide circle pull over the trigger. It was the exact same model type used by the bounty hunter, Josh Randall, on the television western, "Wanted Dead or

Alive". He turned to the mirror, cocked the gun, pointed from his hip at his own reflection, and pulled the trigger, blowing the mirror to pieces and blasting a hole in his closet door. His heart raced as he looked at his destruction. Ace Brinlee was Steve McQueen. Ace Brinlee was dressed to kill. Ace Brinlee was nuts.

Roads End was alive with noises and activity. Dog owners were feeding, watering and settling the dogs they had brought back with them. They would search for the missing dogs later. Hunters like Bill Wood, Leon Barrett, Jimmy Carter, and even young Jimbo Carter, liked finding the dogs as much as they liked hunting the deer. Real hunters find pleasure in all aspects of the hunt and take away lifetime lessons with all that may occur in the hot or cold moments of the hunt.

Half the early arrivals were in the building, lined up holding empty bowls in their hands, waiting their turn for Don Crawford to ladle out his special brew of Texas chili to all those hungry or brave enough to down the first spoonful. He had slices of buttered Texas toast and a assortment of crackers, including saltines, Ritz and even those little rectangular Captain wafers. Don was smiling from ear to ear as he heard the noises the eaters were making as his brew entered their mouths and slid down their throats. Their eyes said it all and he knew the chili was a hit. He did love to see folks chow down with his creations.

Haystacks' eyes opened wide when he saw Raymond Lloyd walk out of the woods and onto Rosier Road about fifty yards away from where he had stopped the truck. His eyes opened even wider when he realized Raymond had a dead deer draped over his right shoulder and a dog under his left arm. The dog looked dead, too. His gun was in his left hand and what looked like, a huge snake was draped over his left shoulder.

Haystacks had never seen such a sight in his life. It was easy to see Raymond Lloyd was something real special. It was easy to see he was most definitely the Meatpacker. He was approaching the truck.

Haystacks didn't want to struggle with getting out of the truck, but he knew he had to meet his friend properly. As the Fatman worked his way out of the cab and onto the ground, Raymond walked to the back of the truck and lifted the dead dog over the raised tailgate. He leaned his gun against the rear bumper and tossed the snake off his shoulder into the back of the truck, too. Raymond then gently eased the dead deer from his shoulder and placed it next to the first deer he had killed earlier that morning. Haystacks joined Raymond at the back of the truck.

"Damn, son, you dropped another one?" Raymond looked up at his huge friend.

"Yeah, but I lost Ben, dammit. I saw when that bastard sunk his fangs in. He hit Ben right behind his ear. I never seen a dog die so fast. The poison must have hit his blood stream faster than normal, 'cause he was dead in half an hour." Haystacks was sad about the dog and he was in awe of the ability of the Meatpacker, but he was also hungry. He had a hopeful question for his good friend and master hunter.

"You ready to head back in? They all stopped huntin'. Too many snakes. Hell, countin' that thing you killed, it's about six or seven of 'em, now. Poor Jimmy Carter lost another dog to the bastards. He loses one 'bout everyday, don't he? And that damn lucky Leon lost a dog and then it came back from the dead. To hear him tell it, every car on the train hit the dog. It was dead then it wasn't dead. You gotta hear Barrett tell it. You ready to go in?" Raymond nodded and he didn't realize how happy his simple little nod made the Fatman. The hunters at Roads End didn't know they needed to eat their fill of Texas chili quickly, because Chuck "Haystacks" Drew was on his way to take his place in the chili line. In fact, he was a chili line.

First Kill

Leon and his two sons stood at their dog pen watching their true miracle dog, Bud Bo. The dog's legs were now steady as he walked around the pen. Bud Bo stuck his nose through the four inch square opening of the fence wire and Ramsey rubbed the dog's nose. Leon touched Ed and Ramsey on their shoulders at the same time.

"Come on, boys, let's let him settle down and rest. Somethin' special happened here today and we were fortunate to be here to see it. I'm hungry. Let's see what smells so good." The Barrett's headed for the chili line.

Bill, John and Hugh Powell were standing at the skinning rack. Bill had just pinned the hind legs of John's beautiful eight pointer to the wooden two-by-four at the top of the rack. They would gut and clean the deer later. Bill Wood watched the excitement in his son's eyes as he looked at his first deer. He knew how John was feeling because the same emotions were flowing through his veins and touching his heart. He also knew there was yet another and final chapter in the saga of one's first kill. The ritual of pouring the blood of the deer on the hunter and smashing the heart, liver, and all the entrails in his hair and face was alive and well at Roads End. Many hunting camps had traditions about the blood of the first kill and the hazing of the hunter. Roads End took the traditional ritual to another level. Bill Wood knew his thirteen year old would face the blood-drenching soon. He also knew John wasn't thinking about what came next, but it was coming. But, for now, the deer would be on display for the others to see until after they ate some Texas chili. They would be the next three to join the chili line.

The members of Roads End were so deep in the traditions of the hunt and the blood drenching, they gave glimpses of the ancient religion of Mithraism. It was a soldier religion calling for manliness and bravery at all times. Just like Roads End. Mithraism stressed good fellowship and brotherliness. Just like Roads End. It excluded women. Just like Roads End. When sacrificing an animal, the warriors were drenched in its blood and covered with the organs of the beast. Just like Roads End. John Wood would soon be the next Roads End warrior to be Mithranized. The "bounty hunter," Ace Brinlee, held his phone to his ear.

"You boys owe me this. I ain't takin' no for an answer. So, get in that truck of yours, go get your ugly cousins and then come get me. If y'all ain't here in half hour, I'll be huntin' you. And bring some guns." He hung the phone up and dialed another number. The phone at the other end rang twice. His brother, Buford, answered.

"Hello."

"Buford?"

"You all right, Ace?"

"I'm fine, now that I got that shit off me. I'm goin' after 'em, Buford. I want you with me, but I'm doin' it with or without you." Buford's end of the phone line was silent. Ace waited a few seconds. "I can't help it. I gotta do somethin'. That's all there is to it."

"You can't kill all those people, Ace. You know that."

"Why not?" There was silence on Buford's end again. Ace waited a few seconds again. "I said, why not?"

"You're talkin' too crazy, now. You're takin' it way too far."

"There's a way to punish people without killin' 'em. Maybe I'll make 'em wish they were dead. Besides, they're the ones who took it too far. I'm gonna take it the rest of the way." Ace hung up the phone.

Jimbo Carter and Little Mac McGehee were sitting together, eating their chili. Little Mac had filled his bowl with crushed Ritz crackers. The front door of the lodge opened and the huge mass of overalls and flesh moved into the building. Raymond "Meatpacker" Lloyd followed Chuck "Haystacks" Drew to the kitchen area.

Raymond was hidden behind the Fatman at first. Then a number of the members saw "his majesty" had returned.

They gave tribute to the Meatpacker for the first kill with cheers, whistles and applause. Little Mac McGehee and Jimbo Carter watched as the Fatman picked up an empty bowl and held it out to Don Crawford, who was still holding the deep ladle. Don filled the bowl with the Texas chili. Haystacks sat down on one of the wooden benches at the kitchen counter, grabbed a table spoon, three pieces of Texas toast and a fistful of assorted crackers. The Fatman attacked the bowl of piping hot chili. Jimbo whispered to Little Mac.

"We gotta change rooms, somehow, I tell ya." Ed and Ramsey sat down across from Jimbo and Little Mac with their bowls of chili. Jimbo looked at Little Mac, smiled and asked the Barrett boys an interesting question.

"Y'all gotta a good bedroom for the night?" Raymond Lloyd was standing against the far wall, eating a piece of Texas toast, when Big John Blanyer walked through the front door and made an announcement.

"I know he ain't mentioned it, but Raymond's got two big bucks in his truck, along with a dead dog, and the biggest damn rattler I ever seen in all my days." A single voice from somewhere in the room yelled out

"Long live the Meatpacker!" The room exploded with more cheers, whistles and laughter as another tribute to the best of the best, Raymond Lloyd. Haystacks stomped his big feet as his way of honoring his friend, but he didn't lift his face away from the bowl and he didn't stop spooning out the hot chili from the almost empty bowl.

The black Ford Cyclone GT stopped in front of Ace Brinlee's single wide trailer. Buford Brinlee stepped out of his car and walked to the door of the trailer. His older, but smaller, brother pulled the door open before Buford had a chance to knock. The brothers were face-to-face.

"Don't come in here, Buford, 'less you're here to help me." Buford didn't respond to Ace's statement as he walked into the house. Ace followed his younger, but bigger brother. "I mean it, Buford. No sense you bein' here if you're gonna try and talk me out of this." Buford looked at Ace.

"I ain't gonna do that. I know once you set on somethin', that's it. So I'm with ya. Tell me what you want me to do." Ace smiled, hugged his brother and slapped him on his back.

Don Crawford had a big grin on his face as he watched the two huge pots of his special Texas chili disappear. He would save a gallon or so for any late comers or for the real chili lovers, later. Maybe Haystacks would make a midnight chili run to the kitchen and Don wanted to have a bowl left for the big eater. The chili was made just for emergencies, such as the hunters coming in early like they did. The real big feed would be later and would consist of roast beef stew over rice with red jacket potatoes, carrots and more big cat head biscuits with real honey. He had also made another one of his popular white icing spice cakes like the one he made for John Wood's birthday. This one was a triple decker sheet cake, would feed an army and had no slant. He had even made a punch bowl full of banana pudding with more vanilla wafers than bananas. Don Crawford set the bar when it came to cooking at Roads End. His culinary act would be terribly hard to follow. The members were spoiled by his catering abilities. They all loved him, but Ace Brinlee hated him.

Ace stepped to his trailer door when he heard a horn blow outside. The horn played an instrumental version of "Dixie." Ace knew, his sometimes friend, Hamp Stone, had arrived. His brother, Buford, yelled from the back of the trailer.

"Ace! How the hell did you manage to tear this closet door up like this?" Ace didn't respond and opened the door to see Hamp Stone sitting in the driver's side of his Dodge truck with the huge tires on it. It was half truck, half swamp buggy. You almost needed a stepladder to get up into it. There were two other men sitting up front in the truck next to Hamp. Ace couldn't see them very well, but he knew they were Hamp's two cousins, George and Howard. They called George, Bulldog. It was obvious to see why they called him by such a nickname. If you were to hold up a picture of the University of Georgia mascot, Uga, next to George's head, the resemblance would be uncanny, right down to the flat nose, baggy cheeks and canine bottom teeth. George "Bulldog" Stone was an ugly man. But, not as ugly as his brother, Howard.

Bulldog's brother, Howard, was called Hatchet. Something happened to his head during birth. It was thin and longer than a normal head like maybe the doctor squeezed the baby forceps too hard. Nobody really knew what happened, but they were sure something bad went wrong. They were an ugly and strange pair, but no more strange than Ace Brinlee.

"I knew you boys wouldn't let me down. We gotta do somethin' first before we get to the real business at hand." Hamp had to comment on the way Ace was dressed.

"What the hell are you dressed like that for? You look like you been invited to militia trainin' with the Klan." Ace had his answer.

"This is the way a man looks when he goes to war." Ace turned around and moved back into the trailer. Hamp turned to Bulldog, sitting next to him. Hatchet was next to the passenger's window.

"That's one crazy, some'bitch." The two cousins nodded in agreement with Hamp's description of Ace Brinlee. They all looked at the trailer door when they heard Ace's voice as he walked out of the trailer, followed by his brother, Buford. Buford was strapped and loaded for bear.

"Me and Buford's gonna ride with y'all. We gotta go out to the end of No-Go Road and get my goat out of that damn wet clay. It ought'a be dry enough, by now." Ace and Buford jumped into the back of Hamp's truck and Ace hit the top of the cab before he sat down, as a signal for Hamp to go. Hamp hit the gas and they were headed to No-Go. They were true commandos from the Whispering Pine Trailer Park, right outside of Woodbine, Georgia. The Brinlees were declaring war on the Roads End hunting camp. Big John Blanyer stepped up next to Bill Wood.

"Bill, you seen Lester?" Bill looked around the room.

"Come to think of it, I haven't seen him all day. Not since breakfast. Hell, knowin' him, he might have gone back to bed. Did ya check his room?" Big John shook his head.

"He ain't in his room. He was with me today. He was at the Lounge. Last time I saw him, he was happy as a clam. Grinnin' like a damn fool. I didn't know the man had teeth to smile with. It was down right creepy." Bill gave Big John a puzzled look.

"I'm not real sure what ya mean, John. Ya sort'a lost me there."

"You do know what happened out there today, don't ya?" Bill had the same puzzled look on his face.

"No, John. I guess I don't. I was so excited about my boy's deer, I guess I missed it. What happened?" Big John changed the subject for a second.

"I wanna see if Lester's car's still out there." Bill followed Big John outside to the concrete slab. They both looked around the front yard. Big John knew where the car was supposed to be parked.

"Well, it's gone. He's gone." Bill didn't understand John's concern.

"John. Lester sneaks off every time he's here. Why does it surprise you so much, this time?" Big John took a deep breath and told Bill the reason for his strange amount of concern.

"Lester hunted with me today, or I should say he was out there with me. As usual he ain't done much huntin'. And actually, that's a good thing. I wasn't too excited about bein' in the woods with him pointin' a gun in any direction. He had one of his terrible headaches and all he did was lay in the back of the truck on a piece of canvas. He really didn't bother me none. I just felt so bad for him. I could tell he was in pain. I did hear him snorin' one time so he did sleep some, but I think he was awake and in pain most of the time." Bill interrupted Big John's story.

"You know how much he drank last night and he has those headaches all the time. The combination of the two, headache and hangover, probably is too much for him to take. It is sad. When Lester's sober and headache free, he's a good man to be with. I like him." Big John smiled and continued his story.

"I like him, too. I'm worried though. Ya see, he fell out of the truck." Bill's eyes widened.

"What do you mean?"

"I mean just what I said. The drunk bastard fell out the back of my truck. Head first in the middle of the road. I was doin' about thirty. I saw him in the mirror. Right over the side of the truck. Head first. Hit the damn lime rock like a dead grouper." Bill's eyes and mouth were open. He had no words as his friend continued. "I just knew he was dead. I slammed on the brakes. I didn't really want to get out of the truck, but I did. He was about twenty yards away. I was scared and expectin' the worst." Big John stopped for a few seconds to give Bill a chance to absorb all his words. He went on. "There he was, face down. Nose buried in the road. He wasn't movin' or makin' any noise. I don't know why, but I didn't run to him. Hell, I didn't even hurry at all. I'm not sure why I walked so slow. I was as scared as I've ever been. He looked dead. When I finally got to him, I could see the white lime rock dust moving from the air coming from his nose. At least he was still breathin'. I got down close to him and said, 'Lester, you all right?' I know that sounds stupid, but that's what I said. Then he answered me. He didn't move or lift his head from the road. He said, 'I'm just fine, John. My headache's gone.' Then he pushed himself off the road with his arms, like he was doin' a push up. He stood up and brushed the lime dust and dirt off his clothes and arms. He took a handkerchief from his back pocket and wiped the dirt off his face. I just stood there, like an idiot, but I didn't know what to say. I finally managed to say, 'Lester, you sure you're all right? That was a nasty fall, you took.' I figured he was hurt bad and didn't know it 'cause he was in shock. He looked at me, smiled and said, 'I'm really fine, John. I'd like to ride up front with you, if that's all right?'" Bill had a question.

"Does anyone else know about this?"

"Oh yeah, most everybody. While you were celebrating John's first kill and Leon's Bud Bo was comin' back from the dead, the rest of us were lookin' at Lester grinnin' like Sylvester when he thinks he's gonna finally eat Tweety. He looked different with that big smile on his face. I didn't even know he had any teeth for smilin'. I guess Lester took that grin to town."

Lester Rowe drove his late model Cadillac down Rosier Road on his way toward Brunswick, Georgia. He still had that big smile and was feeling better than ever with the demise of his headache. His destination was a local VFW lodge that was a haven and regular stable for a number of notoriously loose women. Lester was attracted to women of low moral fiber. He had drinking and women on his mind.

The old Caddy was moving along the dirt road as smoothly as possible when Lester spotted a car sitting in the middle of the narrow road, dead ahead. There was still enough light from the setting sun to see that a young black woman was sitting on the hood of the an old black Mercury. Lester took his foot off the gas peddle and brought his car to a slow stop with the front of his car stopping ten yards away from the front of the other car. He would be careful with the odd situation. He took his pistol from the glove compartment and stood up outside the car with the door opened, but shielding him.

"Hey, little lady. What ya doin' way out here all by ya'self?" The young girl smiled a beautiful straight white teeth smile. Lester noticed how pretty she was, but he was still concerned with his own safety. He took a look around and then looked at the young woman.

She was dressed in a new white dress that fit tightly on her firm young body. She looked to be in her twenties. Her stomach was flat, her legs were muscular, and her breasts were big, round and standing at attention. She definitely had her headlights on and they were high beamers. She was beautiful to look at, but Lester would remain cautious until he was sure his life was not in danger. He still stood behind the car door.

"You gotta admit, little lady, it's kind'a strange you bein' out here like this. This is private property, ya know? You're at Roads End."

"Yes, suh. I was tryin' to take a shortcut back to Nahunta and I got lost. I'm late for my friend's weddin', but now my car just cut off. I was hopin' somebody would come along. It'll be dark soon and I'll bet it's pretty scary out here at night."

"That explains your pretty dress."

"Yes, suh. I won't make it, now. It's way too late. My mama's gonna be mad."

"What happened to your car?"

"I don't know, suh. It just stopped." Lester looked around again.

"You ain't got no big black buck waitin' in the woods to rob me, do ya?" Her eyes widened. She was surprised with his question.

"No, suh! I wouldn't do nothin' like that." She slid off the hood of the car and stood on the ground. She was only about five feet tall, but her body said she was all woman. Lester closed the door and put the pistol in his belt. Her eyes widened again when she saw the gun.

"You ain't gonna hurt me, is ya, suh?" Lester patted the gun as he walked toward her.

"This is just so nobody hurts me. I have no intentions on hurtin' you."

"Well, you don't have to worry about me, suh. I'm just glad to have somebody here with me. Dark's comin' and all." Lester was next to her, now. She was even prettier up close. A pleasant scent filled his big nostrils.

"Damn, girl, you smell good."

"Thank you, suh. I like smellin' good." Her smile was as intoxicating as his Wild Turkey. Lester was excited about the way she looked. He was becoming more confident and he felt safe with the beautiful young black woman.

"You sure are a pretty little thing, ain't ya?" She looked down.

"Thank ya, suh." Lester put his hand on the hood of the car.

"Ya say, she just conked out on ya, huh?" She lifted her pretty head and looked at Lester with her jet black eyes. His heart pounded in his chest.

"Yes, suh. I was movin' along and then it stopped." Lester wanted to eat her like a chocolate Easter bunny. His mouth went dry.

"What they call ya, little lady?" Her smile made Lester's blood flow in all directions.

"I'm Taffy. They call me Taffy." Lester's eyes lit up.

"You mean, like the candy? That chewy candy?" Her smile was the biggest so far.

"Yes, suh. Just like the chewy, golden brown candy." Lester was beside himself. He felt his manliness push against the zipper of his pants. Taffy moved to the door of her Mercury.

"Maybe she'll start, now." Lester was in a trance for a second until he heard her voice.

"Yeah, try to start her." Taffy got into the driver's seat behind the wheel. Her dress went up as she slid into the seat, exposing her tanned thighs. The slit on the side of her new white dress was open and Lester could see one side of her white cotton panties. He was on fire internally. Taffy turned the key and there was only a clicking noise. Lester had heard that noise before. He moved to the front of the car and opened the hood. He looked directly at the battery cable connections.

"I knew it." Lester reached his hand toward the battery. Taffy tried to see what he was doing through the front windshield.

"What is it, suh? Can you fix it?" Lester closed the hood.

"Try her now." Taffy turned the key and the engine fired up. She couldn't believe it. She screamed like a child as she revved up the motor.

"Can I turn it off?" Lester nodded his head. Taffy turned the car off and jumped out of the car. She moved to Lester's side. She was close enough to smell her again.

"You must know all about cars. What was it?" Lester smiled.

"I think this bumpy ol' road got the best of one of the battery cables. It just had to be put back on the stump and tightened, that's all."

"Well, I'd a been stuck out here all night if you hadn't come along. I don't know how to thank ya. I ain't got but four dollars." Lester smiled.

"A woman that looks like you don't never need no money." His comment embarrassed her and she put her head down again. Lester was boiling inside and all the blood had left his head and filled elsewhere. Taffy looked up and saw it in his eyes, then she saw it in the bulge in the front of his khaki pants.

"You wanna touch me, don't ya suh?" Lester couldn't believe

what he had just heard coming from her full lips. He looked into her eyes and then his eyes looked down her body. Her forward and aggressive words took his breath away.

"I like to be touched." Taffy took Lester to another realm when she reached down and felt the front of his pants. "I ain't never seen a white man before. Can I see it?" Lester couldn't move or talk. He was afraid it was the liquor or the fall from the truck. It couldn't be real. Taffy reached out, unbuckled his belt, unsnapped his pants, unzipped his zipper, reached under the elastic waist band of his boxer shorts and pulled out his blood filled handle, exposing it to her eyes and the cold evening air. It could have been ten below and Lester would not have felt the cold. Her eyes widened at the size of what she held in her hand. Lester was in a Taffy pull shock. Her next statement sent Lester into another dimension.

"Let's get in that big back seat in your car. It's gettin' too cold and dark out here. Besides I want to be comfortable when you put that thing of yours inside me." Taffy held onto Lester's impressive manhood as they walked to the back door of his Cadillac. She used it like a leash. He didn't care. In fact, it seemed to steady Lester as they walked. Like her hold gave him balance. Taffy had stirred the animal within Lester Rowe. She released her hold and Lester moved into the big back seat first. Taffy took off her shoes, pulled down her panties and climbed into the back seat with him.

Taffy went right to work. She was a true pleaser and knew exactly what to do and how to repay Lester for fixing her car. The sexual encounter between Lester Rowe and Taffy was not one sided at all. They did things to each other. They did them willingly. Lester loved the way she wanted to do things to him and how she allowed him to do whatever he wanted to her. He had never had such freedom with a woman. Usually there was some kind of restriction when he dealt with a woman, but not with Taffy. She liked it all. She took it and gave it back. When he was rough, she was too. When she was slow and gentle, he was too. When he bit her, she bit him. It was pure animal sex and Lester Rowe didn't want it any other way, but neither did she.

She sat across his lap and took him deep inside her. She turned around and leaned the front of her body against the back of the front seat and allowed him to enter her from behind. Lester had held off as long as any man could. She had taken his best and she had plenty left. When she realized he was going to explode, she moved away, pushed him down into the seat, and took all he had left. It was the ultimate sexual encounter for Lester Rowe or anyone who would have the good fortune to cross paths with Taffy.

Lester still wasn't sure it was all real or not. He had had so many dreams that seemed real enough, but were only dreams in the end. He was waiting for one of his fellow members to wake him from this dream and he would find he was sleeping in one of the bunk beds at Roads End, instead of sitting in the back seat of his Caddy. He lay his head back on the seat and closed his eyes. He could feel Taffy's hand touching him and he could smell her perfume and body fluids. She was still trying to please him. He moved when she touched him because he was still sensitive. He hoped she would wait for him to recover and allow him a second time. He felt he would be even better the second time. He always lasted longer the second time. Lester also thought that if it was real, it would be a secret he would burn deep in his belly. No one needed to know about Taffy and her abilities. Perhaps he would make arrangements to see her on his future visits to Roads End. She could definitely be habit forming. He knew he would even pay her if she asked for money.

The sun was gone and the temperature had dropped considerably. The Roads End members and guests had filled their bellies with Texas chili, spice cake and banana pudding. The beer, liquor and cold drinks were flowing freely. After the wild first day, they were all settling down for an evening of more poker, campfires, stories, jokes, lies and, in some cases, a trip to town or at least to the VFW hall near Brunswick.

Bill Wood, Doc Johnson, Hugh Powell, Big John Blanyer, and Luther Reynolds sat around a big campfire in front of the old cook shack. The shack was only used for storage now that the new building was equipped with a modern galley. The skinning rack was next to the shack with the three deer of the first day hanging side-by-side from the boards on top. Bill Wood stared at his son's first deer. Luther Reynolds watched Bill.

"Would you stop lookin' at that boy's deer." Bill smiled.

"I can't help it, Chief. I just can't help it." Luther smiled and hit Bill on his knee.

"I guess not, son." Billy Crosby and Paul Peavey Jr. stepped out of the darkness to join the group by the fire. They were good looking men. Luther had to say something.

"Now, look at these two pissbirds comin' out of the dark over there. As homely as you two are, I know y'all ain't got no women hidin' back there givin' y'all blow jobs. I hope you two got separate bunks here tonight." They all looked at the young men waiting for a response. Luther had more.

"Now, you boys go inside and splash on some of my Old Spice smell'em on those peach fuzz faces and then you will at least smell like men." Billy Crosby found a bit of courage while standing near the fire with the elders.

"We were hopin' we could sit with you gentlemen and learn from your years of experience and wisdom. Do tell us of the good old days." Luther looked at the others and smiled.

"Damn, I'm startin' to like the hell out of this boy." They all laughed again. "Sit down son, both of y'all. Always enough room for a few more pissbirds."

Lester Rowe opened his eyes. It was dark outside the car and cold inside the car. He knew it had not been a dream because the beautiful young black woman, Taffy, was cuddled up next to him, sleeping. They were both completely naked. He scanned her hard strong body for a second then touched her shoulder. She opened her eyes and smiled that smile.

"I was thinkin' about somethin' you said." Lester looked at her.

"And what was that, darlin'?"

"You called this place, Roads End."

"That's where we are, Roads End. I'm a member here. We hunt here every year." She smiled and sat up exposing her entire body to Lester.

"A few years back there was a story goin' 'round at home about some men from a place called Roads End. You ain't one of them fellas got arrested for skinny dippin' over in the Satilla River near Nahunta, are ya?" Lester laughed out loud at her wonderful question. She smiled as he laughed. "Well, are ya?" Lester roared again because of the serious look on Taffy's face.

"No darlin' I ain't one of those skinny dippers. I wish I had been one of 'em. I was just laughin' 'cause I do know who they are. I just don't know who they were skinny dippin' with." Lester leaned back in the seat and the faces of Jim Mott, Derwin Nall and Tom Cravey flashed in his head. His thoughts of his wild old friends were interrupted when Taffy's words shocked him once again.

"I was waitin' for ya to wake up and I was hopin' we could do it one more time before I had to go."

Ace Brinlee sat at the steering wheel of his purple Pontiac GTO as Hamp Stone used a towing rope and his big blue Dodge Ram truck to pull the GTO out of the ditch and back to the middle of

No-Go Road. The clay was dry and the car moved easily. Ace started the engine, Buford got into the passenger's side of the car and then Ace pulled up next to Hamp.

"Follow me. We'll stop at the power lines off All Night Road. Ace hit the gas and the GTO led the way. Bulldog looked at his cousin, Hamp, as they followed the clay splattered purple goat.

"What's Ace up to, Hamp? I hope he ain't gonna get us all killed out here." His brother, Hatchet, made his face uglier than it already was when he heard the words "get us killed." Hamp was concerned, too.

"I ain't sure. I think it's got somethin' to do with the way they was treated out at that Roads End camp last year. I think that whole situation's been brewin' inside Ace all year. He talks about it all the time. Let's see what he wants us to do before we say anything to him. We'll decide what to do when we know what he wants us to do." Bulldog was still worried.

"Ace ain't gonna let us decide nothin'. I hate owin' him Hamp, but I don't want him mad at me." Hamp nodded.

"Let's just see what happens." Bulldog looked at Hatchet.

"Stop doin' ya face like that."

The campfires and the storytellers were blazing at Roads End. The crowd around the fire had grown to fifteen. Bill Wood had everyone's attention.

"I can't remember his name, but he was somebody's guest. He had long blond hair, like a woman would have. Longer than we were used to, anyway. I have to admit, he was a pretty little bastard." Big John remembered who Bill was talking about.

"That's my neighbor's boy. He's still a pretty thing. They call him Perkins." Bill nodded.

"That's right. We told him to put a hat on when he went to sleep to cover his pretty hair, because if Tom Cravey came in drunk late that night, he might think he's Marilyn Monroe, and climb into bed with him. The poor boy stayed awake all weekend and never dropped his pants when Tom was nearby." They all laughed again. Tom Cravey had something to add to Bill's story.

"When I realized he was so worried about me, I started winkin' at him whenever I caught him lookin' at me. He was a nervous wreck the whole time he was here. I did walk in on him in the toilet once. He was standin' at the mirror with his hair hangin' down his back. He saw me in the mirror and I blew him a kiss and told him he reminded me of Jane Fonda in "Barbarella." He ain't been back." The laughter was the loudest so far that night. Tom Cravey's addition to Bill's story about the pretty blond haired bastard was a classic and would be told at Roads End for years to come. Leon Barrett and his Uncle James, walked to the fire as the laughter was dying down. James had a comment.

"Somebody has to be tellin' lies to make y'all laugh like that." That was the perfect cue for Luther Reynolds to tell another story.

"Well, let me tell a true one, then. I remember the night you drove up in your brand new Oldsmobile 88. You said you had not been drinkin', but anybody who would park their new car across the railroad tracks to see if the train would be able to stop in time, had to be drunk or stoned in some way. James Reynolds shook his head. Billy Crosby did not know the story. He was curious.

"What happened, Mr. Luther?" They were all silent, waiting for the answer.

"Well, son, half the car stayed right out there near the tracks and the other half ended up somewhere at the crossing at State Road 84. James' 88 went to 84." They all laughed again as Leon and Uncle James sat down with the others. Leon sat between Charlie Jefferson and James Carter. He looked at Charlie.

"You seen our boys, lately? I saw 'em all eatin' some cake and then they were gone." Charlie shook his head. Tom Cravey had the answer.

"I saw 'em. They found that box of Playboy magazines in the closet. We boxed 'em up last month when we thought some of the women were comin' out to help with the cleanin'. The women didn't come and the Playboys stayed in the closet, until y'all's little band of horny pimples went on a treasure hunt." Luther Reynolds couldn't resist.

"Look at the bright side, fellas. At least when someone asks you if you know where your children are at night, you can say, 'hell yes, I sure do.' They might have their noses buried in titty pictures, but you damn sure know where they are." The laughter exploded at the expense of the men who brought their sons to be part of the rough language, adult talk, liquor, poker, rattlers, guns, the Meatpacker, and all the other excitement that was Roads End.

Taffy stood outside the back door of Lester's Cadillac. She was cold as she dressed and put her shoes on. She looked into the back seat at her first white man lover. Taffy knew he was dead. She knew the moment he died. She was glad he had finished the second time, but she was sure the second time was what killed him. She took his money, his watch and his pistol. He would have given them to her anyway, if she wanted them. Lester Rowe's last hours on earth were liquor and headache free and filled with incredible sex with a woman of low moral fiber. She didn't even know his name but, Lester Rowe's little black African princess had her '55 Mercury headed back to Nahunta.

Ace Brinlee stopped his clay splattered GTO when he turned onto All Night Road. Hamp Stone pulled his Ram truck up next to the purple Pontiac. Ace got out of his car first. He was still dressed in complete combat gear with the Josh Randall sawed off shotgun strapped to his side. He looked like a road warrior from Thunderdome. Hamp and his cousins hesitated in the truck as they watched the mentally disturbed, Ace Brinlee. Bulldog talked with his teeth clinched and tried not to move his lips.

"Look at GI Joe out there. You do know he's crazy. And he's probably gonna get us all killed." Hatchet turned his long deformed head toward his brother and made another ugly face. Hamp opened the door.

"I know he's crazy, but we do owe him." He got out of his truck. Bulldog looked at his brother.

"You really gotta stop makin' those faces all the time." Buford had joined Ace at the front of the GTO. Hamp walked over to stand with them. He had a moment of courage and he had a concern.

"Ace. We know somethin's really botherin' you. What's this all about?" Ace looked at his younger, but bigger brother. Ace began moving toward Hamp.

"It's about revenge. It's about payin' folks back. It's about settlin' scores. It's about payin' debts. It's about sat-is-fact-ion." When Ace said, "Satisfaction", he was almost nose-to-nose with Hamp. Hamp didn't like it and he backed away. Ace looked at Hamp's truck. Bulldog and Hatchet were still sitting in the cab.

"Would you tell them two mutant relatives of yours to get out here and quit hidin' in that truck like rats." Hamp motioned for his two cousins to get out of the truck. They jumped out and walked to where the others were standing. Ace watched them as they approached.

"It's nice of you two goons to join us." Hamp didn't like Ace's comment toward his cousins. Ace could see that Hamp was mad. It showed on his face. Bulldog looked like a bulldog, so Ace didn't know if he was making a face or not. Ace did know Hatchet was making a face and he had to comment.

"Holy shit, boy. You gotta stop reactin' to things by makin' a face. You really do." Ace turned to Hamp. "Now, I know these two can't help makin' faces, but I don't think I like the one you made just now." He stepped closer to Hamp. "I get a strange feelin' you and your boys don't want to help me here today. Let me refresh your memory." Hamp didn't like Ace Brinlee standing in his face, but he didn't move back this time as Ace gave him his reminder. "These words are from your mouth. 'Anytime you need us, Ace, we'll be there for ya.' Do you recall sayin' that?" Hamp didn't move.

"I know what I said, Ace. I'm here to help you. When you called, you didn't have to threaten me. I was comin'. You don't have to talk to us like we're one of your dogs."

The anger building in Ace Brinlee was easy to see as they stood toe-to-toe and nose-to-nose. Hamp Stone was not a coward. He could hold his own if he had to. He was leery to challenge Ace Brinlee because of his reputation, but if he had to he would defend himself. Hamp Stone found another moment of courage.

"We came here to help you and do what you want, but you ain't told us shit. It's like you're playin' a game with us. So, tell us what you want and stop all this crazy stuff." Ace Brinlee didn't like Hamp's aggressive tone. His eyes widened and his heart pounded in his chest at Hamp Stone's challenging words. Hamp knew his words had angered the crazy one. It surprised Hamp when Ace stepped back away from the stare down position. But, he was even more surprised when Ace pulled the sawed off shot gun from his side and pointed at Hamp's head. Hamp was frozen with fear. His two cousins made the worst two faces of the night up to that point, but there was still plenty of the night left. Ace didn't say anything. He just held the gun a few inches from Hamp's trembling lips. Buford stepped up next to Ace.

"He's right, Ace, you're actin' crazy. That's our friend, Hamp, dammit. We've been friends since school. Please put the gun down." The stare continued. "Ace, don't do this. Hamp don't deserve to be treated like this and you know it." Ace held the gun in place.

"Ain't nobody talkin' to me like that no more." Buford had to try.

"So, you're gonna shoot Hamp 'cause of some words. You ain't mad at Hamp. Put the gun down." It was obvious that Ace thought if he put the gun down he would appear weak and he continued to hold the gun up. Hamp made it easier for him.

"Ace. I don't want to die here today. I need a better reason to die." In Ace Brinlee's warped mind Hamp's words were like a plea for mercy and he considered that a victory. He lowered the gun and ended the stare with his old and now former friend. No man can forgive another man for such a threat. Hamp knew he would hate Ace Brinlee from that moment on. He would pay his debt that night, if he could, but that would be all he would ever do. Ace strapped the sawed off shotgun to his leg and turned toward the others.

"Buford says I can't kill all the members of Roads End." The three Stones looked at Buford and then at each other. Ace went on. "I say Buford's probably right. Buford says I can't kill Bill Wood and Leon Barrett." Hamp's eyes lit up. He knew both men. "In fact Buford says I can't kill nobody out there. I say, 'why not'?" They were all silent. "I ask you, boys. How does a man get revenge, settle scores and get sat-is-fact-ion, without somebody dying?" No one answered. Ace had the answer to his own question.

"I'd decided to get my revenge and satisfaction by inflicting pain and suffering. I've decided to punish one evil man for the deeds against me by many. I have chosen one to represent them all because he has been the worst of the offenders. And you boys are gonna help me bring this man to the painful fate he deserves. When I have him in my hands you can go about your boring redneck lives and your debt will be paid. I want Leon Barrett to bleed. I want Leon Barrett to cry for mercy. I want Leon Barrett to beg for my forgiveness. I want Leon Barrett to know who is inflicting the pain on him." Ace paused for a second and seemed to be thinking to himself. Hamp found courage to speak up, once again.

"You want us to help you kill Leon Barrett?" Ace turned toward Hamp.

"I realized last night that killin' him don't make him suffer. I want him to remember me in his nightmares. He can't have nightmares about me if he's dead. I just want him to wish he was dead." Hamp looked at Buford.

"You goin' along with this?" Buford didn't change his facial expression.

"I'm with my brother." Hamp looked at Ace.

"What do you want us to do?" Ace smiled.

"I want you boys to help me get him out to the old fish camp and get him into the smokin' shed, where they smoke mullet and hang deer up for smokin'. I want Leon Barrett hangin' in that shed like the deer he hangs on the skinnin' rack." They all had wide eyed looks on the there faces, even Buford. Ace continued. "I ain't askin' y'all to do nothin' to him. That's my job. I need you to help me find him in the woods or somewhere and take him to the shed. When he's there, you go on home and forget the whole thing." Hamp knew one thing.

"It ain't gonna be easy to find him alone tonight or even away from the camp. And it ain't gonna be easy to take him when we find him." Ace knew that too.

"If we all watch the camp tonight and get close, he might show and we take him. He could go into town. Hell, he could already be in town. We just have to wait. If we don't get him tonight, we'll get him when they hunt again in the mornin'. If we don't get him then, we'll get him on the road when he leaves, but we'll get him. There's five of us and one of him. I don't care how bad he is, he ain't that bad"

The fireside stories ended when another cold, unexpected rain shower began dowsing the flames of the campfire and the fun of the stories. The now group of seventeen would continue their tales of days past at Roads End in the warm, dry comfort of the main building. Don Crawford would be serving his roast beef stew with all the extras at seven and that was only ten minutes away. They all brushed the dirt and mud off their feet when they walked up on the concrete slab in front of the door and went in to join the lodge dwellers who had chosen to stay inside. As soon as they all were inside, the rain stopped.

There was a four man poker game at a small table near the fireplace. The high rollers were not in the dollar limit game. Malcolm Johnson, Ned Smith, Foy Peavy and Elbert Hysler didn't care about the low stakes. They were enjoying the tempo of the game and the good company and fellowship. The aroma from Don Crawford's kitchen filled the rooms. He was the best of the best. He was the "Meatpacker" of the kitchen.

All activities stopped in the building when two familiar sounds touched every ear in the room. First the sound of another train whistle pierced the early night air as they felt the vibration of the train as it passed in front of the main gate of the lodge. The second sound was that of a shot gun blast directly outside the front door. There was a great commotion outside. The gun went off again. The dogs started howling and barking. The sound of an engine roared outside as lights flashed through the front windows, as if the train had rolled up onto the concrete slab. The sound of the engine was like thunder and the building seemed to vibrate. Two more shotgun blasts stopped anyone from stepping outside to see what was happening. Then a familiar voice cut through the tense air the commotion had created inside the lodge.

"I think there's been a damn train wreck out here. Anybody know where James Reynolds' new car might be." Most of the members smiled a smile of relief when they heard the voice coming from the other side of the door. The door opened and their late and long lost member, Derwin Nall, entered the building holding his smoking barrel shotgun. His three sons, Jimmy, Rusty and Vance followed their father into the room. The Nall family had arrived just in time for dinner at the Roads End hunting camp.

The dirty purple Pontiac GTO drove up slowly with no lights on and parked in the woods about fifty yards away from the camp. Hamp Stone's big blue truck stopped behind the GTO. They all got out of the two vehicles and stood together. Ace looked at the front of the lodge building through a pair of binoculars. He scanned the front area from the dog pens to the concrete slab and back again.

"The rain must'a run 'em in or it's supper time. We need to spread out and see what we can see. If you see him come out or he leaves, come tell me. I know it's a long shot, but who knows. He might just fall right into our hands."

Derwin Nall was shaking hands with his friends and fellow members. He introduced his sons to the hunters who had not met them yet. The oldest, Jimmy, liked to drive Bill Wood's white Volkswagen with the deer antlers on top. He had seen the little car outside when they arrived. He walked up next to Bill.

"Hey, Bronco Bill. How ya doin', sir?" Bill smiled at the young man's manners and the fact he called him "Bronco".

"I'm doin' good, Jimmy. I'm always good when I'm at Roads End. I got the bug with me. Did ya see her out there on the side?" Jimmy Nall grinned a big one at the fact Bill Wood mention the little car first.

"Yes, sir, I saw it. She sure is fun to drive." Bill knew what Jimmy Nall was thinking about.

"My friend, Hugh Powell, brought the Bronco in for me. If you want you can use the bug in the morning." Jimmy Nall's face lit up. Bill Wood was a good man.

"Yes, sir. I'd like that. Thank you." Luther Reynolds had been listening to their conversation. He had to make a comment, as usual.

"The boy thinks he's gonna park it under one of those white oak trees Bill planted fifteen years ago, and the dumber deer will think it's a big fat white deer feedin' on them acorns. They'll just walk up to join him and the boy will pick 'em off. The boy thinks Bill's beatle bug is a damn deer decoy." The hunters within hearing distance laughed. The old pissbird could make them laugh. Jimmy Nall had to laugh too, but he didn't care what anybody thought. He still wanted to drive the white Volkswagen with the deer horns on top.

Don Crawford stepped to the middle of the main room and announced, "Supper's ready and help yourself." The hunters didn't mind lining up at all. It was a serve yourself setup with food items distributed all over the galley area. Luther Reynolds spotted the three young single bucks who had gone to town the night before. They were hurrying to eat and they were dressed for another night on the town. Clayton McKendree, Scott Milligan and Bruce Couey were at his mercy once again.

"Holy shit, would you look at these three pissbirds again tonight!" The three young men looked at each other as they were beginning to eat their food. "Why would you three put yourselves through this humiliation two nights in a row? Just stay home and play with yourselves. You know that's a sure thing. Or play with each other, but please don't go out there again." The three young men were always good sports and respectful. Clayton "Hollywood" McKendree had a confession to make.

"Mr. Luther, you were right about that cologne I had on last night. It only attracted flies. I thought I'd try some of that Old Spice of yours tonight and see if I can do better. If that's alright with you?" Luther's face lit up.

"I'm startin' to like this boy more and more every time I talk to him." Luther made them all laugh again.

As the hunters were filling their plates, another group of young fellows entered the main room from the hallway where the bedrooms were located. It was Little Mac McGehee, Jimbo Carter, Ed and Ramsey Barrett, and last, but thirteen, John Wood. They had just finished their Roads End Playboy pictorial festival and now, since they had filled one hunger, they were hungry for food. Tom Cravey spotted them first. Jimbo saw Tom smile and he knew what was coming next.

"Well, well. If it ain't the titty patrol. Y'all been sniffin' them pages, ain't ya?" All eyes turned to the five young men. Their faces were all beet red. Tom Cravey had his victims on the ropes and he wasn't about to let them off easy. He had more for the young men to endure, especially Jimbo Carter. They were at Tom's mercy.

"Now, Jimbo, there's a professional "puddin' puller," even at his young age." Jimbo felt like his heart fell to his stomach. " He knows how to keep warm and he damn sure shares his secret with his friends, don't ya, boy?" Most of the members knew the story about Jimbo's masterbational past. Jimbo felt the room shake with human laughter, but that could have been him trembling inside. The boys were too hungry to run for cover, so they were prepared to take whatever the members were ready to dish out. They were becoming true future members of the Roads End hunting camp. They joined the others in the food line.

Ace Brinlee stood in the dark next to his GTO. He held his binoculars to his eyes. He saw no human movement near the camp. He focused in on the front door, hoping Leon Barrett would walk out, get in his truck alone, and drive somewhere, anywhere. Buford Brinlee had worked his way into the woods to the North side of the building to watch from there. Hamp Stone and his two cousins were at the back of the building. Hamp thought it was better they stayed together. The army of hunters at Roads End had no idea they were under surveillance and they were almost surrounded by the Whispering Pine Trailer Park militia.

The three young and handsome pissbirds had eaten quickly so they could head to town. The VFW would be their destination because Saturday night was the best night for the area women to come out in force. Clayton McKendree didn't really splash any of Luther's Old Spice on as he prepared to leave. Hollywood was only trying to keep Luther from continuing his verbal assault on him and his two friends. He just hoped Luther didn't ask to smell him, but he wouldn't put it past the old man to give him a big sniff before he left. Luther hardly ever missed anything and he saw the three Casanova's at the front door.

"Alright now, boys. Hollywood, you've got to make us all proud tonight. If you bring a woman back with you, don't make it that one who wants to come here all the time. She'll be waitin' on y'all. Don't tell anybody where you're from." Clayton looked back at Luther with a puzzled look on his face.

"And what woman is that, Mr. Luther?"

"You know. The one Tom Cravey brought back here a few years ago. The one with a body like Venus and a face like a mule." They all laughed again. Tom Cravey went along with Luther's humor.

"I remember her. Bein' with her was like ridin' a mo-ped. She was a lot of fun, but I didn't want nobody to see me ridin' her." Tom Cravey was the greatest. The room exploded with howls of true belly laughs. It was the one liner of the night. Tom was in rare form. The three Don Juans left the building while the laughter continued.

Ace Brinlee saw the light from inside the building when the door opened and the three young men walked out. He looked through his binoculars to see if it was Leon Barrett. He recognized the three men who walked out onto the concrete slab. He could see

Barrett was not with them. He watched the three climb into a truck and drive away though the main gate.

The three Stones were still together in the thick woods behind the building. Hatchet was asleep leaning against a small water oak tree. Bulldog was smoking a marijuana cigarette and not looking toward the house at all. Hamp was behind a bush relieving himself a few yards away from the other two. The three Stones wouldn't have noticed if the building was on fire, much less if somebody left. Buford joined Ace at the GTO.

"It's gettin' colder, Ace, and Leon's probably in for the night. Let's forget this stuff and go find the women. It's Saturday night." Ace didn't look at Buford.

"First of all, I ain't got no woman. She went back home to Mayport. She's gonna get her old job back dancin' at the Seclusion on the beach, somewhere." Buford didn't know that information.

"She tell you that?"

"No. I tried to call her and one of her friends was there for some reason. She told me. Hell when I finish with Barrett, I just might hunt her down next. You can go on home if you want and take those idiots with you when you go. I'm waitin' for it to happen. It can't happen if I'm not here. I like bein' a bounty hunter." Buford had no reply for his deeply disturbed brother. Buford moved closer to the car.

"Well, I'm gonna get in the car and get warm. If I fall asleep, wake me if you need me." Ace turned away as Buford got into the back seat of the GTO. He put his binoculars up to his face again. There was a noise coming through the woods to his right. Hamp Stone stepped out of the dark woods. Ace wanted him on watch duty.

"Where you goin'?" Hamp stepped to his truck.

"Ace, it's gettin' colder by the second. I've got a blanket and extra coats in the truck. We're gonna stay 'til this is done, but we're not gonna freeze." Ace turned away as Hamp got the items he needed from the truck. He didn't see Buford in the back seat of the Pontiac. Hamp left with the blanket and coats. He didn't speak to Ace.

Bulldog Stone took the last drag of the small roach left of his joint. Even though he was smoking, he still felt the cold. Hatchet was still sleeping by the tree. There was a noise in the woods near Bulldog and he turned, hoping to see Hamp returning with the blanket and coats.

"It's about time, Hamp. I'm freezin' out here. My damn feet are gettin' numb." Bulldogs eyes opened wide when he heard a strange voice coming from the darkness.

"If you don't put your hands up into the air, so I can see 'em, you're gonna be numb all over." Bulldog had all his senses. One marijuana cigarette did not do very much to him. He focused his eyes on a man walking out of the dark woods.

"I said get your hands up high, so I can see 'em. I won't tell you again." Bulldog's hands went up over his head when he saw that the man had a shotgun and it was pointed directly at him. Bulldog Stone didn't know it, but he was getting ready to meet the "Meatpacker".

Little Mac and Jimbo sat at a table and watched Haystacks eat his weight in roast beef and biscuits from across the room. They looked at each other and had the same thought at the same time. "We gotta change rooms." Bill Wood walked outside with his son, John, to take another look at John's first kill before they settled in for the night. Leon and his two sons, Ed and Ramsey, walked outside, too. They wanted to check on Bud Bo one more time and make sure the other dogs were all right.

Ace Brinlee's heart jumped in his chest when he recognized Leon Barrett, his object of revenge, through the lens of the binoculars. He followed Leon and the boys to the dog pen where what he saw next was a shocking sight. Raymond "Meatpacker" Lloyd walked from behind the building with the Stone brothers walking in front of him. Raymond was holding the shotgun on them as they walked toward the dog pens. Bill Wood and Leon Barrett saw them, too. Leon stepped to assist his friend.

"What ya got here, Raymond?"

"You boys stop here." Bulldog and Hatchet stopped. "I ain't sure yet, but I think there's another one somewhere." Raymond poked Bulldog in the back with the barrel of the shotgun. "This one thought I was somebody else when I came up on 'em. He called me Hamp." Bill Wood stepped up to stand with Leon.

"Hamp?" He stepped closer to Bulldog. "You don't mean Hamp Stone, do ya?" Bulldog didn't answer at first. Raymond put the gun to the back of his neck.

"The man asked you a question and don't make him ask you a second time." Even under the stressful situation, Bulldog had what little wit he had about him.

"Yes, sir. We was just waitin' on Hamp to come back and get us. He got mad at me and my brother, and put us out up front. We been drinkin' and smokin' and I guess we got on each other's nerves. I thought that was him comin' back to get us." Bill Wood had more questions.

"Why y'all in the woods out back?" Bulldog was thinking fast.

"We were gonna see if y'all might help us, but when we got up near the door we chickened out. Somebody was drivin' in and we just ran around back. We didn't mean no harm, sir. We've just had too much to drink tonight. Hatchet smoked another weed and fell asleep. We're really sorry if we caused any trouble." Ace Brinlee had Buford standing next to him as he watched the interrogation near the dog pen.

"Can you believe those idiot assholes have got caught and are talking to Wood and Barrett. They have to be the dumbest sons-ofbitches to ever walk this earth. I should have known better than to trust them to do anything right." Buford turned when he heard a sound as Hamp Stone walked out of the woods with a panicked look on his face.

"Bulldog and Hatchet with y'all?" Buford looked at Hamp and Ace turned to them both.

"Not even close. The two dumb bastards are down there with Barrett, probably singin' like the chickenshit canaries they are." Hamp looked toward the camp. Ace handed him the glasses.

"Here. See for yourself." Hamp took the glasses and looked through them. He saw his two cousins walking toward the lodge building with Barrett, Wood, Lloyd and the three young men behind them. He gave the binoculars back to Ace.

"You don't have to worry about those two talkin'. They ain't gonna say nothin'." Ace had his doubts.

"They'll be spillin' their guts and you know it. They probably already have."

"You're wrong about that. I gotta go get 'em out of there." Hamp turned to get into his truck. Ace stepped toward him.

"And just how are you gonna do that." Hamp got into his truck.

"I don't know, but I'll think of somethin' when I get down there. The sooner I get down there the better for us all." Ace let Hamp go.

All the hunters looked toward the front door when it opened and the Stone brothers walked into the room followed by a shotgun and the rest of the group. The room went silent. Leon took the floor.

"Meatpacker got number three and four. He just ain't killed 'em yet." Hatchet made one of his patent unusual faces. Luther Reynolds couldn't resist.

"Good God, son. What kind'a face is that. You look like the

dog's been keepin' you under the porch." The men laughed, but Hatchet and Bulldog didn't. Raymond took the floor.

"They were out back smokin' weed and this one was sleepin'." Luther couldn't resist again.

"Well, I can understand that. This son-of-a-bitch needs all the beauty rest he can get." There was more laughter, but not from the two captives. Bill Wood joined in.

"They say, Hamp Stone threw them out of his truck up front and they got scared to come in and get help. They say they've been drinkin' and smokin' and made a mistake in comin' here. They were hiding until Hamp came back for them." There were a few groans and some mumbling in the room. Don Crawford stepped out of the kitchen and joined the group.

"That's Bubba Stone's two boys. That one's George and that one's Howard. Hamp Stone is their cousin. These two boys don't cause too much trouble. They smoke too much of that weed and drink too much, but I ain't never heard of them causin' bad trouble. What you two doin' out this way?" Bulldog knew what to say.

"We just got drunk and me and Hatchet pissed Hamp off. He made us get out of the truck as we were goin' by here. He probably stopped here 'cause he knew we could get help and get home." Hatchet turned to Leon Barrett.

"You Barrett, ain't ya?" Leon nodded his head. Bulldog tried to cover for the strange question.

"We've heard 'bout you, Mr. Barrett, from our daddy. He says y'all used to go to the Georgia games together. He loves them dawgs. That's why he calls me Bulldog." Luther Reynolds couldn't help it.

"That ain't why he calls you bulldog, boy." There was more laughter at the expense of the Stone brothers. The lights of a truck pulling up to the front door shined through the front window. Hamp Stone stopped his Dodge next to the concrete slab and jumped out of the truck. He knocked on the front door. Bill Wood was the closest to the door. He opened it to face Hamp Stone.

"Evenin' Doc Wood. I'm really sorry to bother you, but I'm lookin' for my cousins. You ain't seen 'em have ya?" Bill Wood opened the door to reveal Bulldog and Hatchet to him. Hamp's eyes widened when he saw that Raymond still held his shotgun on his two cousins. He looked back at Bill Wood.

"What did they do, sir?"

"We ain't sure what's goin' on, but it's pretty strange findin' them hidin' in the woods out back." Hamp stepped deeper into the room. Bulldog and Hatchet eyeballed him. Bulldog was still being smart under extreme pressure.

"I told 'em you wouldn't stay mad at us long and you'd come back. Sorry 'bout actin' like we did. You know I can't drink and smoke. I always get to actin' stupid." Hamp understood.

"Don't worry 'bout that. What y'all do here?"

"We ain't done nothin', but I guess we was trespassin'. We should'a come in and told 'em we was here, but I wasn't thinkin' too good. I'm better now." Hamp looked at Leon Barrett.

"Mr. Barrett, they don't mean no harm. I shouldn't have left 'em out here. I was drinkin' too and well, it just shouldn't have happened. We're sorry if it caused you folks any trouble." Leon nodded. Raymond Lloyd lowered his shotgun and Don Crawford took the floor.

"Hamp, you boys hungry? We got plenty." Ace Brinlee took the binoculars down from his face and turned to his brother, Buford.

"Now, all three of the morons are inside with Barrett and the others. Just how stupid is this Stone family?" Hamp, Bulldog and Hatchet Stone were all sitting down and enjoying a nice hot meal with the hunters at Roads End.

Hollywood and the other two Casanovas had found their way

to the VFW near Brunswick. The same destination Lester Rowe had on his mind earlier that evening. They had taken a different route to the hall and didn't see Lester's Caddy parked out at the end of Rosier Road. No one would find Lester that night.

The VFW had a standing room only capacity crowd. It was just what the young men were looking for. Music, dancing, beer and women. As they made their entrance into the big wooden floor dancing hall, Hollywood McKendree turned to his friends, Scott Milligan and Bruce Couey.

"If ya see the woman with Venus' body and a face like a mule, you can take her out to the truck. You just can't take her back to the camp." They all laughed and started their hunt for two legged does.

Ace Brinlee was still watching the front of the lodge. It had been at least thirty minutes since Hamp Stone had entered the building. The front door opened and Ace watched the three Stones walk out and get into Hamp's truck. No one else came out of the building. The Dodge Ram pulled away from the concrete slab and headed out through the front gate, turning on the road away from where Ace and Buford were hiding in the woods. Ace motioned for Buford to get into the car. Ace jumped behind the wheel, started the engine, didn't turn on the lights, and went after the Ram truck.

The bellies of the Roads End hunters were full once again. The smell of that after-supper coffee filled the rooms. The younger men were helping Don Crawford with the kitchen clean up. There was a group of storytellers near the fireplace. The card game had moved to the big round wooden table and the four man game had expanded to six players. Luther Reynolds had changed his roll for the night and he was going to be a spectator for a little while and then he was going to bed early so he could rest and be alert in the morning for the deer he didn't get that first morning. The hunters were all settling down for the night and it wouldn't be long before they were all in one of the bunks.

Hamp slammed on his truck's breaks when the purple Pontiac GTO passed him and forced him off the main road. The GTO stopped and Ace Brinlee jumped out of the car. Hamp got out of the truck to meet him.

"Where the hell are you goin'?" Hamp didn't back up as they were eye-to-eye again.

"We couldn't turn your way, Ace. They could have seen us and thought somethin' was strange." Ace looked into the truck.

"What about those two. What happened in there. Did y'all join the, 'let's talk about Ace party'."

"They didn't say nothin' about you to nobody. We stayed in there so it wouldn't look like we were scared. They did good by you, Ace. Nobody thinks anything. Your name wasn't even mentioned. But, we ain't goin' back there tonight. Do what ya gotta do, Ace, but I'm takin' these boys home." The stare continued for a few seconds. Hamp had more for the evil eyed Ace Brinlee.

"I can promise you, Barrett ain't goin' out anywhere tonight. I'll meet you at the fish camp at six in the mornin'. If Bulldog and Hatchet want to come with me, they can. I heard Barrett tell his boys he wanted them to hunt together in the mornin' at the poacher's stand and he wanted to be alone at the beehive stand. Now, that beehive stand is way on the other side. In fact it's the closest stand to the fish camp. You can see the top of the old smoke house from that stand. He's gonna be right where you want him and you just have to wait for him to get there. I'll help y'all take Barrett in the mornin' and then the debts paid in full." Ace nodded his head. Hamp turned and climbed back into his truck. He started the engine, backed it up to clear the GTO and pulled away.

The first day of hunting, drinking, eating and laughing at

Roads End hunting camp was coming to an end. The kitchen was clean. The only noise and movement was coming from the poker game that could very well last until morning. John Wood was tired from the excitement of his great birthday and he told his father he was going to go to bed so he could get up early and go after that second deer. Bill smiled and hugged John at the hall entrance. He did love that boy.

"I'm about ready for bed myself. I can't take all this excitement like I used to." John smiled and went to his bedroom. As John entered the room he was surprised when he saw Ed and Ramsey Barrett sitting on the bunks that Jimbo and Little Mac had used the night before. He smiled when he thought to himself that his two former roommates had tricked the two newcomers into taking their beds and they went to another room. John smiled at his new roommates.

"Hey Ed . Hey Ramsey. Y'all sleepin' in here tonight?" They both nodded. Ramsey answered.

"We had the room on the train side, but Jimbo and Little Mac asked us to trade with them and it didn't matter to us." John smiled, nodded and looked at Haystacks' yellow stained Mason piss jar. He didn't bring it to their attention.

The frightening noises from Dallas Thomas' nasal passages filled the hall and echoed through the entire building. Unless you were deaf, drunk, or unconscious, you could not sleep while Dallas, the king of snore, was snoring. It just so happened that a number of the members were deaf, or drunk, and sometimes unconscious, so there was always somebody sleeping through the infamous, "death rattle." Lester Rowe was one of the members who never complained about the death rattle. He was usually under the influence of Wild Turkey. Lester Rowe would not hear Dallas' death rattle that night, or any other night. He had already heard his own. Arthur Padgett was another member who was not troubled by the rattle. He would just turn his hearing aid off when the death sounds began.

Bill Wood put his hands behind his head against his pillow and stared up at the bottom of the mattress of the top bunk above him. He listened to the sound of the death rattle as he had done many times before. Bill didn't know his son, John, was also staring at the ceiling above him and listening to the sounds of the death rattle. As long as Dallas Thomas slept nearby, the members of the Wood family would not get very much sleep.

Bill Wood let his thoughts take him back in time as he remembered one of the other legendary expert snorers and his good friend, Edgar Masters. Edgar was one of the most colorful characters to grace the hall at Roads End. It has been said, "the best way to know another man is to go hunting or fishing with him. It doesn't take long to recognize and separate the real men who do their share of the work." Edgar was always the first to offer a helping hand in any situation, without any hesitation. Bill visualized the time he saw Edgar hanging like a monkey as he labored to build the highest tree stands in the woods. All the members benefitted from Edgar's tireless and unselfish efforts and hard work, as well as the generous way he shared what he had built with the other members. Bill missed his good friend and he enjoyed his return to the past. He thought about Edgar when ever he climbed into one of those high tree stands. The sound of Dallas Thomas choking brought Bill back to the present and the reality of Roads End. If he wasn't going to be able to sleep, he didn't mind the old Roads End memory flashes.

John was still awake. He wasn't sure if Ed and Ramsey were still awake, too, but he thought they were. He knew Haystacks was still somewhere in the building and the Fatman would be joining them sometime during the night. He was right. Haystacks walked into the room. John looked over at the other two bunks on the other side of the room. He could see Ed and Ramsey's eyes opened wide, looking like big round coins and shining from the moonlight. The huge man filled the room as he turned and maneuvered himself into the bottom bunk under John. The concrete blocks under the bed frame supported his massive weight as he sat down to take his boots off. John was prepared for the foot fumigation. He reached under his pillow and pulled out Luther Reynolds' bottle of Old Spice cologne. He took off the cap and held the bottle up to his nose.

Ed and Ramsey Barrett were not prepared and took the full blast of the unbearable foot odor the Fatman's day of hunting could produce. Ramsey gagged and put his head into his pillow. Ed held his nose as long as he could, but when he could hold it no longer he had to take a deep breath to fill his lungs. That was a huge mistake. There was no good air to breath. Ed and Ramsey had no idea the foot odor was just a small sample of what would come later in the night when the chili, boiled peanuts and cabbage began processing in the Fatman's stomach. They would survive the awful sleepless night surrounded by bodily function noises they recognized and some they didn't recognize and they would never make a deal with Little Mac and Jimbo ever again.

It was still dark outside when the wonderful aroma of bacon, biscuits and morning coffee filled every nook and cranny of the Roads End hunting lodge. The aroma was a welcome treat for Ed and Ramsey, but they were more excited when Haystacks rolled out of bed to be the first one to indulge in the morning culinary delights. Ed, Ramsey and John Wood had heard the noises made when Haystacks was filling his Mason piss jar twice during the night. John had experienced it before, but the sound of urine hitting the bottom of a Mason jar in the dark, was new for the two Barrett boys and they didn't sleep much at all, if any.

Don Crawford had been up and working for an hour. He

already had a special stack of pancakes for his fat friend. Don was a great cook and he enjoyed taking care of his many friends. It didn't take long for the smell of the coffee brewing to bring the Roads End hunters out of their beds and onto their feet. The hallway, latrine and kitchen came alive as the hunters prepared for another day in the woods. Derwin Nall and his three sons were up and ready. They had missed the first day of the season, but they were planning to stay a few days after the weekend. Jimmy Nall wanted to remind Bill Wood about him using the Volkswagen during the hunt.

"Doc Wood, you still O.K. with me using the little bug? I was thinkin' 'bout goin' on out early, ahead of the rest." Bill nodded and smiled at the polite and eager young man.

"She's all yours, Jimmy, but ya gotta talk to Leon about goin' out early and where he's gonna put ya. He's the huntmaster. He says who goes where." Jimmy Nall nodded back to Bill.

"Yes, sir. Thank you for the bug." Bill smiled as Jimmy went to find the huntmaster.

The tables, counters and chairs were full of hunters eating, talking, laughing and raring to go. Big John Blanyer walked up to Leon Barrett.

"Lester was hunting with me yesterday, but he ain't here now. I don't think he came back from town last night." Leon shook his head.

"He probably found one of his Brunswick lady friends. But, you know, he could be passed out in his car somewhere, sleepin' it off. He's been known to do that from time-to-time. Maybe we'll see him, maybe we won't." Leon Barrett stepped to the middle of the room.

"Listen up, men. We'll meet at the Lounge for a break at noon, if you want to come in. We won't go out there first. With the huntin' cut short yesterday we need to get on out there and get after 'em. Some of us have to go on home tonight. I'm gonna ask you to keep the same stand you had yesterday. If someone wants to change with you, that's up to you. Please, just let me know." Leon looked at Jimmy Nall. "Jimmy here's gonna head out there, now. He missed yesterday and he's fired up. He'll be at the far end of All Night Road. He says he likes it way out there." A voice in the crowd hollered, "He'll damn sure be alone 'cause ain't nobody goin' out that far to see him." Jimmy smiled. He wanted to be alone. Luther Reynolds couldn't resist.

"Hell, we all need to go out there with the boy. How we gonna get any deer up this way when he's drivin' the decoy?" They all laughed again. Bill Wood threw Jimmy Nall the keys to the bug. Jimmy was out the door.

Ace Brinlee leaned up against his purple Pontiac GTO. It was still splattered with the red clay from No-Go Road. The car was parked next to the old mullet smokehouse near the fish camp. His brother, Buford, sat on the hood of the car. Ace still had his "Wanted Dead or Alive" bounty hunter, road warrior look from the night before. Ace didn't change his expression when he saw a set of headlights coming toward them on the dirt road leading to the fish camp. He knew it was Hamp Stone's truck.

The white Volkswagen with the deer horns on the top was the first vehicle to go out through the main gate that morning. The other trucks and Jeeps would soon follow. The woods would be full of trucks, Jeeps, dogs, hunters, perhaps a few snakes, and the Whispering Pine Trailer Park militia.

The big blue Dodge Ram truck drove up next to the front of the smoke house. Ace saw Hamp at the wheel, but his facial expression changed when he saw a strange sight with Hamp in the truck. Bulldog and Hatchet were sitting in the front seat and they were wearing black knitted ski masks over their heads. Hamp stepped out of the truck. Ace looked into the cab. Bulldog and Hatchet stayed seated and looking straight ahead through the front windshield. Ace looked at Buford. Buford shrugged his shoulders and shook his head. Ace turned to Hamp who had walked closer to the GTO. Ace had to ask.

"What the hell are those two idiots wearin' those masks for?" Hamp looked back at the cab and then back at Ace.

"Ace. They have to be in character for this caper of yours. They wanted to be the tag team wrestlers called the Assassins. Besides, they don't want Barrett to see 'em." Ace didn't know what to say. Hamp wanted to tell him more so he would understand. "Ace, listen. These two are here to help you make this happen, like we promised. They don't want to be recognized." Ace was frustrated with the two fools.

"Are they afraid I'll recognize them, too. Do they have to wear them now. Can't they put them on later. They're idiots, Hamp." Hamp tried to explain.

"They need to stay in character, Ace. They'll come through for you, but it has to be their way. I've got a mask, too. I don't want to be recognized, either." Ace was even more frustrated.

"But, you don't have yours on already, Hamp. Tell them to take those things off. They look ridiculous sitting there with them on."

"Why can't you just let 'em be. We'll take Barrett down when it's time. What do you care if they wear those masks, or not?" Ace looked at Buford. Buford could only shrug his big shoulders again. Ace looked back at Hamp.

"Then tell them to stay in the damn truck until we move. I ain't gonna let them walk around out here lookin' like that." Ace turned to say something to Buford, but he stopped when he saw another set of headlights on the road that passed the smoke house. They all heard the lawn mower sounding engine and saw the white Volkswagen fly by, headed away from the fish camp. It was still dark and they didn't think whoever was driving the little car was able to see them.

The tree stands and blocks of hunting territory were filling with the eager hunters. Leon was the last to leave the camp. He would drop Ed and Ramsey off at the poacher's stand and he planned to work the beehive stand for a few hours and then go back to hunt with his boys. He gave Bud Bo the day off, but another family favorite, Big Jake would lead the pack.

Ace Brinlee entered the old smoke house to see where he would prepare a place for Leon Barrett. Buford Brinlee made sure Ace was out of sight and turned to Hamp Stone.

"You don't have another one of those masks do ya?"

The small shed had a wooden table to one side. It was once used for cleaning the mullet and skinning the deer before they were smoked. There were racks hanging above where the fish and meat would hang while it was being tenderized and smoked. Pieces of rope and leather were still tied to the long piece of wood in the top of the shed. Ace Brinlee wanted Leon Barrett to be in that small shed. He didn't care if he was on the table or hanging from the rafters.

Jimmy Nall had his hunting day planned. He wanted to hunt and be alone away from the others. He felt there were too many disruptions the year before and he wanted to concentrate on the hunt and not the foolishness. He liked being a real hunter and not a weekend woodsman. He slowed the bug down and turned off Shingle Mill Road, rolling the beatle car right next to one of Edgar Masters' highest tree stands in the last block. It would give him a great look across the field and into the woods around the stand.

He had his gun, ammunition, food, water, even a Nehi orange soda. He was ready to settle in and start his day in the woods. Jimmy had told his father not to expect him to go to the Lounge at lunch for all the beer drinking and playing. He was going to hunt and that was all. His words were, "Don't look for me 'til dinnertime and maybe even later."

Jimmy took his survival supplies up into the tree stand first. After he had placed them where he wanted, he went back down to the little car and got his gun. He didn't want to carry anything with the gun. It was the safe thing to do. He stood high on the platform and looked out over the field across the road. Jimmy laid his gun on the wooden floor of the stand, picked up his canteen of water and leaned back against the tree the stand was attached to. He turned the canteen up to his lips and the back of his head rubbed against the tree. As his head touched the tree, Jimmy Nall thought his face had burst into flames. His head, neck and face were instantly covered with bees. He had put his head into a huge nest of yellow jackets and they covered him like a scary mask. Every bee on him, stung him. The more he fought the more they attacked him. The pain was excruciating and unmatched in his life. He took his coat off and rubbed his face with it. Jimmy's leg muscles seemed to give way under him and he stumbled to the edge of the stand. He tried to get to the side ladder, hoping the bees would not follow his descent. He missed the first step.

Jimmy Nall was airborne and falling toward the ground below. When he hit the ground he heard a bone snap on impact. He was on his back looking up at the tree stand above him. The bees were still stinging him, but not in the numbers as before. He reached for the painful spot on his leg. His hand was covered with blood. Jimmy Nall looked at his leg and saw he had suffered a compound fracture and his thigh femur bone was broken and it had gone though his skin and dungarees. The pain of the bee stings was overshadowed by the awful pain from his leg. He was scared to move. He couldn't if he wanted to. His gun and supplies were up in the stand. It was seven o'clock in the morning. Jimmy was at the last tree stand. He had told them not to look for him. He lay his head back on the ground. Jimmy Nall was in shock. Leon Barrett watched his son's, Ed and Ramsey, walk toward the poacher's stand.

"You boys be careful and take care of each other. I'll be back in two hours." Leon hit the gas peddle of his truck and he was off to his favorite beehive stand. The year before he had dropped a deer on the short side of the O'Quinn and he was hoping for the same results as before. He had the same thoughts as Jimmy Nall. He would hunt alone. He was a real hunter. He had no idea what lay in store for him at the old mullet smokehouse.

All of the Roads End hunters stopped and listened when they heard the first gun shot of the second day. Billy Crosby was standing near the power lines and he had just killed his first deer, ever.

Ace Brinlee walked out of the old smokehouse. Hamp and Buford were standing near the GTO. The masked Assassins were still sitting in the truck. Ace looked toward the truck and shook his head. Then he looked toward Buford and Hamp.

"I want him hangin' in there, like a big fat buck. We might just smoke his ass." Hamp had to make his position clear.

"We're gonna help you get him here and then we're gone. We ain't killin' or cookin' nobody." Ace glared at Hamp.

"You don't have to tell me that again, Hamp. I know the deal. We need to go." Ace stepped to his car. "Follow me, Hamp. I'm gonna leave the goat on the other side of the road. We'll all go in the truck and park it in the woods behind the tree stand. When we take him and knock his ass out, we'll blindfold him. He won't see the truck." Hamp didn't like it, but he got into his truck and followed the red clay speckled Pontiac GTO to the road.

Jimmy Nall was still on his back looking up into the tree stand above him. His face was swollen from the hundreds of bee stings and the breathing passage in his throat was almost closed off by the swelling. He couldn't yell for help or move at all. He had heard Billy Crosby's first shoot, but he knew it was from a long distance. He could only hope someone would come his way. Jimmy heard a noise and turned his head the best he could to see where it came form. He saw a big buck and two doe standing next to the white Volkswagen. The decoy had worked.

Hamp Stone backed his blue Dodge Ram truck into the woods near Leon Barrett's beehive stand. His two masked cousins sat next to him and the Brinlee brothers were in the back of the truck. Ace tapped on the truck window and motioned for Bulldog to hand him the ax handle Hamp had sitting in his gun rack in the truck. Bulldog handed the ax handle out the side window. Ace took the wooden handle, jumped out of the truck while it was still moving, and stood on the ground beneath the tall wooden tree stand. Hamp backed the truck deeper into the woods and out of sight before the others got out and walked to where Ace was standing. Ace was nervous and his adrenalin was flowing.

"We don't wait. We take him down the second he steps out of the truck. He won't expect it at all, but we can't wait." They were all nervous. The two masked Assassins were wide-eyed and breathing heavy. Hamp was concerned.

"Where you want us, Ace?" Ace looked at Hamp as to say, "Hell, I don't know", but he didn't say it.

"Just get somewhere we can come from all sides so he can't run nowhere." Buford was quiet and looking down the road. Ace stepped to his younger, but bigger, brother.

"He'll come. Don't worry." Buford looked at his older, but smaller, brother.

"I ain't worried about him comin' or not. I'm worried about what's gonna happen when he does come." Buford turned away from Ace and looked down the road again. Ace didn't like Buford's comment.

"Don't you get jittery on me now. I got enough squirrels to deal with." Ace turned and looked at the Stone brothers. They were standing side-by-side, shoulder-to-shoulder, looking straight ahead, like frozen wide-eyed statues. The sound of a motor somewhere on the road started five hearts pounding at once. Buford knew it was Leon.

"He's here. He's alone." Hamp reached into his side coat pocket and took out his knitted ski mask and put it over his head, stretching and adjusting the material until his eyes and mouth filled the appropriate holes. Bulldog and Hatchet moved back away from the tree stand and squatted down behind a thick group of Palmetto fans. They could not be seen. Hamp moved to the thicket to the right of the stand. Buford left the edge of the road and stood behind the tree attached to the beehive stand. Ace's eyes widened when he saw Buford take another ski mask out of his coat pocket, and put it over his head. Buford looked through the eye holes in the black knit mask. Ace was shocked.

"You, too?" Buford reached into his other pocket, took out another mask and threw it to Ace. Ace caught the mask, and as the sound of Leon's truck came closer, Ace Brinlee hurried and put the mask on his head. He became the fifth Assassin. He took a hiding place near Hamp Stone.

Jimmy Nall reached to his belt and took out his big hunting knife out of its leather sheath when a huge rattlesnake moved past him. Before he could get the knife out the snake had moved on. It was just passing through. Jimmy's eyes were slowly closing from his cheeks and eye lids swelling. He could hardly breathe, he couldn't move and he would soon be blind from the swelling. He could see the three deer still standing next to the white Volkswagen with the deer horns on top.

Leon Barrett drove his truck off the road and stopped next to the beehive stand. He couldn't hear the five hearts pounding in the woods near him. If he had heard them, he would have never stepped out of that truck. Leon opened the door of his truck and stepped out onto the ground. He looked up into the tree stand above him and then he looked at the ladder boards nailed to the tree to be sure they were still there.

Buford, Hamp, Bulldog, and Hatchet waited for Ace Brinlee to make the first move. Ace felt they had already waited too long. He could only hope the other masked Assassins would keep their part of the deal and follow his lead. Leon had his back to Ace when he gripped the ax handle and moved quietly and quickly from his hiding place. Leon felt Ace's presence and he saw a shadow as Ace came up behind him, but it was too late. The flat side of the ax handle hit Leon in the neck and back of the head.

Leon saw the dreamlike quivering around his eyes and an electric shock went through his body. He fell forward against the tree which kept him from falling to the ground. He found the strength to turn and face his attacker. The masked Ace Brinlee swung the ax handle again and Leon lifted his arm, catching the end of the wooden stick in the grip of his strong hand. Ace Brinlee's eyes almost popped out of the knitted holes of his mask when Leon pulled the ax handle out of his hand. Ace stood there and stared at the huge Leon Barrett. Leon was hurt and dazed from the first blow to his head. Ace Brinlee couldn't believe Leon Barrett held the ax handle in his hand.

Buford Brinlee came from behind the tree and grabbed Leon in a bear hug. As soon as Leon felt Buford on him he threw his head backward connecting the back of his head with Buford's nose. Blood exploded from Buford's nose and he released his grip. Leon swung the ax handle, but missed Ace. Hamp Stone was the next masked Assassin to join the assault.

Leon was still standing. Ace was in front of him. Buford had recovered and he stood to Leon's side. Hamp moved from his hiding place and stood to Leon's other side. Leon was still dazed as he looked at the three masked men standing on three sides of him. His quivering eyes tried to watch each one, but he was too weak.

The three attackers were not sure what to do next. He had not gone down so easily. Leon needed to gain some recovery time. He looked at the new arrival.

"When you gonna take your turn?" Leon took a defensive stance, holding the ax handle and waited for their next move. It came from the bloody nosed Buford. He charged at Leon with his head down to tackle him off his feet. Leon lifted his knee and it connected perfectly with Buford's already broken nose. The blood splattered all over Leon and Buford. Buford fell straight down to the ground at Leon's feet, like the ton of bricks he was. Leon swung the ax handle down and hit Buford on the top of his head. Buford Brinlee was no longer in the fight. Ace Brinlee stepped back and pulled the sawed off shotgun off his side and pointed it at Leon.

"I thought we could do this without just killin' you outright. I should'a done this when you got out of the truck. I went soft 'cause I was with these idiots." He looked down at Buford. "I can tell he's hurt bad. He don't never stay down. I was just gonna punish ya, but now I do have to kill ya." Leon looked at the masked Hamp.

"I ain't seen y'all's faces. You ain't done nothin' yet mister. You ready to be part of killin' a man?" Ace didn't look at Hamp. He walked closer to Leon and held the gun even higher, aiming directly at his face.

"He's already part of it." Ace Brinlee took off his ski mask and revealed himself to his victim. Leon didn't change his facial expression.

"I want you to know who's blowin' your head off out here in the woods. This bein' your favorite spot, and all." A new voice joined the conversation.

"If you pull that trigger, you die. If you turn around, you die. If you don't lower that gun by the time I stop talkin', you die. Now, put the gun down." Ace lowered the gun to his side. Ace saw

Leon Barrett's eyes light up like flashbulbs. The new voice continued with more instructions. "Put it down on the ground easy like you're puttin' your baby sister down." Ace bent over and put the scatter gun on the ground. "Now, turn around real slow like, or you die." Ace turned slowly to the voice. His eyes widened to their fullest when he found himself face-to-face with the Meatpacker.

"You all right, Butch?"

"I am now, you handsome bastard." Raymond Lloyd smiled.

"Ain't I though." Meatpacker walked to Ace Brinlee and without hesitation hit Ace in the side of his head with the butt end of his shotgun. Ace went down and didn't move. Raymond turn to Hamp.

"Take the mask off." Hamp's eyes widened. Leon stepped to his friend. Then looked at Hamp.

"Leave it on, mister." Raymond's eyes lit up.

"He can't be part of this, Butch, and then just walk. That'll be a mistake." Leon put his arm around Raymond's neck and pulled him toward him touching their foreheads together in thanks and respect.

"It ain't no mistake. Let him go." Hamp's eyes were their biggest. He looked at Leon then at Raymond. He wasn't sure what to do. Leon helped him with his decision.

"If you ever tell about this, we will finish it. Tell the other two." Hamp Stone swallowed and turned away slowly, hoping he wasn't going to become another kill by the Meatpacker. Leon looked down at Ace Brinlee, but addressed his question to his friend.

"How'd ya know." Raymond smiled.

"I didn't. I wanted to cross over instead of goin' around and I ran right into Ace's ugly purple car. It's parked about a hundred yards over there." Raymond pointed across the road. "I thought it was awful strange for that car to be that close to where you were gonna hunt. I just came to check on ya." The sound of a truck

Nose-to-Nose

engine starting came from the woods. Hamp Stone would find a way out of the woods without driving past Leon and the Meatpacker. Hamp looked through his back window into the bed of his truck. Bulldog and Hatchet were lying flat on their backs, side-by-side, looking straight up into the sky, still wearing their masks. They were headed home. Raymond Lloyd stood over Buford Brinlee.

"Butch, I think this one's dead." Leon nodded.

"For some reason I thought he was. The way he fell and didn't make a move or a sound. I thought he was dead." Raymond stepped to Ace Brinlee and turned him over using his foot. Ace Brinlee opened his evil eyes and saw Leon Barrett and Raymond Lloyd standing over him. He smiled.

"I was gonna cook you and eat you for supper." Leon took the gun from Raymond's hands.

"Like I told ya Friday night; nobody's gonna miss y'all, nobody's gonna look for y'all, nobody's gonna care about y'all."

A pack of Jimmy Carter's running dogs chased the three deer away from the white Volkswagen. Jimmy Nall heard them. He just couldn't see them. He also heard a single shotgun blast coming from the direction of the old smoke house. Most of the hunters, including Ed and Ramsey Barrett, heard the same single shot. James Reynolds turned to Dallas Thomas when he heard the shot.

"It's probably that damn Meatpacker, droppin' another one. He always seems to be in the right place at the right time. I'm gettin' hungry. I think we ought'a put out the Lounge call for anyone who wants a cool one." James Reynolds smiled.

"You won't have to ask me twice." Dallas Thomas made his call over the radio.

"If you're interested. All roads lead to the Lounge. I know it's early, but what the hell."

Leon Barrett's truck drove up to the poacher's stand where Ed and Ramsey were located. They were both on the high perch when the truck pulled up. Their father stuck his sore head out the window of the truck.

"Like Dallas said, 'It's early, boys, but I just thought we'd go on over to the Lounge. There's a cold Nehi for y'all and a cold beer for me." The two boys smiled and climbed down the tree ladder.

The Lounge was filling up with vehicles and hunters as it had done many times before. Billy Crosby had the first and only deer for the day, but it was early and they would drive the dogs again and again. Bill and John Wood stood with Hugh Powell watching the trucks roll into the Lounge. Bill Wood did love that boy, John, and all the excitement that made Roads End. Leon Barrett drove into the Lounge with Ed and Ramsey sitting in the truck cab with him. He was glad to be with his sons. Leon would never realize how close he came to being smoked like a mullet. He was right about the Brinlees. Nobody would ever find them, because nobody would ever look for them. Jimmy Nall would suffer for eight long hours before his father would find him. But, he would be found a full two days before anyone found Lester Rowe. Only Taffy, from Nahunta, and the buzzards knew where to find Lester. It was just another weekend of hunting at Roads End.

In Memory of Jim Mott
The Ambassador to Roads End